I0590177

Callahan's Cottage

Judy Lannon

Copyright © 2025 Judy Lannon

All rights reserved.

This is a work of fiction. All names, characters, businesses, places, and incidents portrayed in this book are products of the author's imagination or are used fictitiously and are not to be construed as real. Any resemblance to actual events, organizations, places or persons, living or dead, is entirely coincidental.

No part of this book may be used or reproduced in any manner whatsoever without written permission from the publisher or author, except as permitted by U.S. copyright law.

Paperback ISBN: 979-8-9985537-0-7

Ebook ISBN: 979-8-9985537-1-4

Published by Outer Beach Press

This book is dedicated to all the dogs in my life.

Thank you for patiently waiting, with the promise of a walk, while I typed and paced and typed some more until I typed the final The End.

To Puck and Truffles; Mike, Oliver, Roxie, Skyler, and Rudy; Ace and Tia; Diaz and Mo; and Jersey and Hampton.

And to Maverick, the coolest cat, who never waited for anything!

Acknowledgments

I want to thank all my fellow authors who have served as my sounding board, encouraging me to keep writing, especially when I wanted to give up.

Thank you to Robert Harrison of Seneca Author Services for his patience, guidance, and some handholding throughout the process of releasing Callahan's Cottage out into the world.

I Go Down to the Shore

"I go down to the shore in the morning an depending on the hour the waves are rolling in or moving out, and I say, oh, I am miserable, what shall—what should I do? And the sea says in its lovely voice: Excuse me, I have work to do."

— Mary Oliver, A Thousand Mornings

Chapter One

"I hate writing, I love having written."
— Dorothy Parker

Ellenor

"**B**ack in the day, it was easier to kill someone and get away with it."

"So that's the first line of your next book?" The words are practically growled from the other end of the line.

Despite the whitening strips on her teeth, Ellenor lights a cigarette and inhales deeply. *I hate this.* "Yes, that's the first line." She moves to her next idea and starts again. "The rage of the ocean dragged her down to the murky depths below, surrounding her in darkness."

"Jesus, Ellenor, are you just making shit up on the fly? You are a goddamn award-winning author. I expect a lot more from you."

Clearly, Ellenor Snow and her agent, Maggie O'Hare, are not on the same page.

Ellenor hesitates, then she gives it her last shot. "As a child, I watched my mother sort out her pills each evening after dinner. I particularly liked the blue ones, but she didn't seem to have a preference. I began stealing those when I was in the first grade—she never noticed. I don't know why I only stole the blue ones. According to my therapist, I harbored a subconscious belief that she would return to me once she ran out of the blue pills."

"Now, *that's* what I'm looking for. *You*. I'm looking for you, and now you're channeling your Southern inner child. Go with that. Let's meet at The Front Porch later today. You got me in the mood for some gumbo and a good, strong Hurricane. We can discuss more of your ideas for this book. You do have more ideas, don't you? And I recently finalized your book tour, so we can go over that. Let's say four this afternoon? See you then." Maggie hangs up before Ellenor can agree or disagree.

Ellenor puts out her cigarette and peels off the white strips as she looks down at the yellow legal pad where she just scribbled three potential openings for her next novel. *My Southern inner child? I'm about as Southern as Mary freaking Poppins. I have saltwater running through my veins— a Cape Codder through and through. And my inner child ran away when I left the Cape.*

Ellenor steps into her shower, the hot water shocking her senses for a moment before she adjusts the temperature. She stands under the rain shower head, wishing she could get out of drinks and a heavy late lunch with Maggie.

Today is supposed to be her Let's Begin Again Day— healthy food, no carbs, no sugar, no alcohol. She lathers her short blond hair with her store-brand shampoo, wondering how she has come to this point in her life. She finally rinses off, steps out of the shower, and applies Dove moisturizing cream to her sinewy arms and legs.

It's three o'clock, and Ellenor still doesn't have a good excuse to get out of meeting Maggie. She has a few ideas, but they're as lame as her attempts at the opening lines for her next novel. She could tell Maggie she's "in the zone" and can't come up for air, that she has already written fifty pages this afternoon. But then Maggie would insist on seeing those fifty pages.

Maggie and Ellenor are close in age, but the two couldn't be more different in their appearance and demeanor. Maggie radiates an air of self-confidence and has a street-smart attitude that sets her apart. Her poise is something Ellenor is acutely aware of, and this awareness only serves to emphasize Ellenor's self-perceived shortcomings, making her feel awkward and inadequate—the extreme opposite of Maggie.

Maggie is also fastidiously punctual—not a second before, not a second after—while Ellenor is perpetually late. Begrudgingly, Ellenor changes from her sweats into an oversized white knit sweater and a pair of her "dressy" jeans. *I don't remember these being so tight.* She lights another cigarette and calls an Uber. *I should walk—it's not that far. But it could rain...* That settles it. She takes her umbrella to show no one in particular that, though she could walk, she shouldn't because of the chance of precipitation.

Ellenor hesitates a moment just inside the double glass doors of The Front Porch. She's surprised to see how busy the local spot is at this time of day. She notices a good share of hipsters, business suits, and what she refers to as the

"Pilates Set"—women who are effortlessly beautiful, in perfect shape, and can fit in anywhere.

Ellenor sees Maggie first and instantly regrets what she's wearing. She unconsciously runs her hand through her hair, cut in a no-muss-no-fuss style, grateful she at least combed it after her shower. Maggie is leaning against the bar, laughing and talking to a handsome older man. Ellenor reminds herself to stand up straight as she slowly places one black Converse sneaker in front of the other, tugging at her sweater and wishing it could make her disappear.

Maggie spots her and waves. She makes her way through the afternoon bar crowd, turning heads in her vibrant hot-pink A-line maxi dress that accentuates her tall frame and slender waist. Her long wavy platinum-blond hair adds a touch of urban chic to her overall look.

"There you are. Come on, our table's ready."

They sit by the window, sipping on rum Hurricanes while Maggie does most of the talking.

Maggie rummages through her black leather briefcase and hands Ellenor a manila folder. "Here's a copy of your book-tour schedule. I emailed it to you and updated your calendar on Gmail, but I thought you'd like a hard copy. Jill has made some notes, and once everything is finalized, I'll shoot that over to you. Don't look so forlorn—there's a surprise this time. Look at the location of the last stop on the tour." She is obviously pleased with how the tour is panning out.

Ellenor reviews the schedule, this time paying attention. "The Nantucket Book Festival? This is probably the most prestigious book event on the East Coast. There are some big-name authors who speak there. Writers like Jodi Picoult and Geraldine Brooks. How did you do this? I've tried to get into this festival for years."

"That was before you were a multi-award-winning, best-selling author who is lucky enough to have one of the best literary agents in the publishing world. Your star is rising, Ellenor Snow. You keep going like this, and I'll have you on *Oprah*."

"I don't think she has a show anymore."

Ellenor's mind is churning. *Nantucket. Dare I do this? How can I not?*

Maggie is staring across the table, eyeballing Ellenor. She takes a sip of her drink. "What is wrong with you? I thought you'd be happy about this. Maybe even a little excited. I'm sorry if I sound perturbed, which is unprofessional, but I'm worried about you. I need you to be on the top of your game for this tour."

Now it's Ellenor's turn to take a sip and look at her agent-slash-friend. "Look, I appreciate all the work you—or should I say, Jill and your team—have put into organizing this tour. But Nantucket? You do know it's within spitting distance of the Cape."

"What's wrong with that? Cape Cod, your childhood home. What did you say? Something about a small fishing island with a big drinking problem? That's good. Put that in one of your books."

"I'll give that some thought. Here comes our food. And Maggie, you don't need to worry about me. Let's stop talking shop."

Over coffee, Ellenor brings up the tour again. "It's a

long tour—six weeks. But it might be nice to take some time off and extend my stay on the East Coast for a bit." As if talking to herself, she adds, "This would be a good reason to ditch Charley."

"Ah, Charley. I didn't know he was still in the picture. You're right, this might be a good reason to chuck Chuck."

They both start laughing. Ellenor is struck by the realization that she's forgotten the simple, unadulterated pleasure of a good laugh, to simply let go. *Why don't I laugh like this anymore?*

She walks back to her condo in the Castro District, hoping to both burn some calories and clear her mind. The book-tour schedule and conversations about it have rattled her. Six weeks is a long time to be away from home.

Once back inside her condo, with the door double-locked, Ellenor makes a cup of tea. She can't shake her reaction at the mention of Nantucket and the Cape—a disquieting sensation that refuses to dissipate. She kicks off her sneakers, finds her journal and a pen, and curls up in her favorite chair, a luxurious chaise lounge upholstered in sumptuous chocolate-brown velvet. Perfectly positioned, the chair provides breathtaking views of the Golden Gate Bridge to the left and Dolores Park to the right.

She picks up her journal and begins to write.

April 9

Met M @ Front Porch. Great food and Hurricanes. The walk home nearly killed me. Buzz Kill Hill is brutal after two drinks, hence the name. I got my spring/summer book tour schedule. Talk about brutal. I'll be gone for six weeks—and people wonder why I don't have any pets. This go-around, it's the East Coast, starting in West Palm Beach. Then up the coast, Savannah, Charleston, DC, Newport, RI, and ending on Nantucket. Most of these stops have at least two events each. I can handle this, but Nantucket is a big red flag for me. Only thirty-six miles of ocean separating me from home. It's weird that I still think of the Cape as home. I haven't been back there since Mom died. I'll be so close it would be stupid to not go see Dad, but do I really want to do that? Picture this: What if I have a kid I haven't seen in five years, and they're nearby but can't be bothered to visit me… talk about awful! But I don't have a kid, so what do I know about parenting? Dad probably wouldn't see it that way. Out of sight, out of mind.

I could use a vacation—maybe I can get a cottage on Nantucket, maybe in Sconset. A sweet, rose-covered cottage overlooking the ocean. No internet, no cable, just quiet solitude. I'm always alone, though, so why would I want that kind of vacation? But if I was on Nantucket, I could take a quick flight to the Cape, visit with Dad, and fly back to the island. It would be nice to catch up with Delle and Red. Nantucket's better than staying on the Cape—the last thing I want is to run into people I don't want to see. This way, I'm far enough away, but I made the effort. I can hear him saying, "Jesus, Ellenor, flying here? Too good for the ferry, huh? Oh, look at Ellenor, the writer, all high and mighty now." Maybe I'll vacation anywhere but the East Coast.

It seems I have a lot of maybes. Note to self—change the locks and then chuck Chuck.

"What do you think of this one?" Maggie holds up a tasteful Donna Karan sleeveless dress in a black-and-cream floral. "I love it."

"Maggie, you are a brilliant agent, but you're clueless about what I like to wear."

Maggie sets the dress aside as her chocolate-brown eyes lock on Ellenor.

"Clueless, Ellenor Snow? How many years have we known each other? I'm sure you have no idea. We have known each other for almost eight years. I'll have you know, I pay attention. You like to wear jeans, T-shirts, and sneakers. If it's chilly, you might throw on a hoody. That's fine if it works for you, but it won't work for this book tour. You're going to be in affluent seaside resorts. Try to be more like the author with the fake red hair who sells all those wildly popular beach reads—readers love her. She knows exactly what her readers expect. She embraces that and dresses the part."

"I don't write beach reads; I'm not a redhead, and I am not wearing that stupid flowery dress you're holding."

Maggie sighs. "Ellenor, you are exasperating. But I don't give up easily. Follow me."

She walks with a sense of purpose out of the shop's front door and into the boutique down the block. Ellenor hurries to keep up with her. Before she realizes what's happening, Maggie has cornered a salesperson and is telling her what she wants in different sizes.

"Maggie," Ellenor hisses, "have you looked at the prices of this stuff? This T-shirt is $300. That's ridiculous—it's probably made by slave labor in China."

Maggie just glares at her. The look says *not another word out of you*. By the end of the shopping trip, Maggie has bullied Ellenor into mix-and-match outfits for the book tour. The wardrobe combines a collection of T-shirts in black, white, and cream with wide-leg cotton trousers in the same color palette. Maggie added a structured black blazer, a classic white blazer, and a Kate Spade vintage jean jacket to finish off the wardrobe. To solve the shoe dilemma, Maggie chose two pairs of Torey Burch leather trainers, one white and one black, along with a pair of navy-blue boat shoes. Maggie also included a statement outfit to finish the tour on Nantucket—a navy-blue-and-white-striped Ralph Lauren oxford shirt with Prada white linen pants. The new clothes say *Ellenor Snow belongs on this tour.*

Maggie holds up a simple crossbody phone bag, saying over Ellenor's objections, "I respect your 'I don't carry a purse' mantra, but nobody is going to carry your credit cards and phone for you. Unless you have another suggestion, I strongly suggest you take this one."

Ultimately, Ellenor admits—only to herself—that she doesn't hate what Maggie has chosen. She almost feels attractive in them—almost. The cost of the shopping spree makes her want to vomit, though, even with reassurance that *it's a write-off, darling.*

Ellenor steps back into the dressing room and takes a moment to look at the woman in the mirror, noticing the subtle differences that make her feel like a stranger to herself.

She flashes back to her freshman year at Nauset High School. Ellenor Snow, the daughter of a fisherman and a waitress at Safe Harbor—not the most prestigious restaurant in town. The older girls seemed fixated on making her life miserable. Over the summer, Ellenor had transformed from an ugly duckling into a stunning blond beauty, leading them to tease and taunt her relentlessly once school began. With all the negative attention, the older boys started showing interest in her, which only made matters worse. Ellenor was beautiful, quiet, and mysterious in high school. She was—and still is—thin and tall at five-foot-six. By the time she hit puberty, her body said *look at me, how amazing is this!* Ellenor loved her cascading blond hair, even though it had a mind of its own, some days straight and other days wavy. Her deep-blue-gray eyes, the color of an angry ocean, are fringed by long jet-black eyelashes and thick dark-brown eyebrows that accentuate her high cheekbones. The last day of her freshman year marked a pivotal moment for Ellenor. She took a pair of rusty scissors from her father's truck and chopped off her beautiful hair that fell to her mid-back. This dramatic change was followed by her decision to wear her brother's old flannel shirts to hide her body—an attempt to disappear.

Ellenor shakes her head to rid herself of those memories and exits the dressing room. "I'll take everything, please," she says to the salesperson.

Chapter Two

"Everything is hard before it is easy."
— Goethe

Emma

April in New York City can be cruel and, at the very least, fickle. Winter and spring weather are completely unpredictable, with surprisingly warm days followed by unwelcome snow, sleet, and biting cold.

"Alright, let's try it again. Turn to the left and position yourselves face-to-face. Try to remember why you're marrying each other," says Emma Callahan.

Emma is freezing. The bride is turning purple, and the groom looks miserable. *Serves them right. Who in their right mind gets married in early April in this city? Why in God's name do they want their wedding pictures taken in Central Park?* Her pants are dirty from kneeling on the cold, damp ground, her fingers are numb, and yet there she is— "Smile, good. Turn, that's it. How about just the bride now?"

Sixty minutes later, Emma is warming up inside the Tavern on the Green at the wedding reception. She has changed into a pair of black pants and exchanged her Doc Martin work boots for heels, her down jacket for a black cashmere turtleneck. Years of outdoor photography sessions have taught her many tricks, and a change of clothes is paramount.

"That's a much better look for you," Grace says sarcastically.

Emma and Grace joined forces years ago, combining their photography skills to create their business, E&G Photography.

"Next April, I'll do the outdoor photo shoots, I promise."

"I hope I'm not doing this next year," Emma mutters.

"What?" Grace looks up from fiddling with her camera.

"Nothing. Come on, we still have plenty of work to do. You get the flower girl. I'll handle the groom's mother."

In Emma's professional assessment of humans, depending on the age, a flower girl can be more difficult than the mother of the groom. She adjusts her black camera bag on her shoulder and goes in search of something to eat before looking for the mother of the groom. She sits in the back of the Tavern, absentmindedly picking at an overpriced appetizer. The clinking of glasses and animated laughter from the elegantly dressed, slightly inebriated wedding guests fill the air as she watches them celebrate. She observes the newlyweds. *You poor fools. If you're lucky, you might make it, but there's a better chance that, over time, the warm glow of love will fade away and the slow unraveling of the marriage will begin to eat away at you until there is nothing left.* In Emma's case, though, the end of her marriage was anything but slow. One day, her husband stopped loving her. Just like that—goodbye, good luck, the end.

Emma stands in the red glow of the safelight, surveying the black-and-white photographs she gently pulled from the stop bath tray and hung to dry, her jet-black hair piled messily on the top of her head.

"Knock knock."

"Grace?"

"It's me. Is it safe for me to come in?"

"Sure."

Grace cautiously opens the door to their studio's darkroom as Emma studies the pictures from the shoot at the Tavern on the Green. Emma loves this part of the business. In her opinion, the process of developing film is as close to Zen as you can get. Grace doesn't have the patience to follow the necessary steps to recreate the photo shoots for their clients. She prefers working with digital cameras. Looking at it from a business angle, the logical choice is to embrace the convenience of instant review and the simple editing offered by a digital camera. They both know darkrooms are becoming obsolete, but they both agree nothing can replace the rich and subtle gradations that quality film provides. For now, they balance both options the same way they balance their business and friendship.

"What do you think?" Emma asks.

"I think they're good. Very good. The Tavern-on-the-Green couple should be happy."

Both Emma and Grace struggle to remember their clients' names—they remember the location, the day, and how the shoot went, but not the names.

"Great. I'm so happy for them," Emma says cynically.

Grace runs a hand through her straight brown highlighted bob, looks up at her, and says what few would dare.

"Honey, it's been five years since your marriage broke up. I think it's time you stop being so bitter."

Grace's comment surprises Emma. She thought she was doing a good job of masking the remaining fallout from Ethan's betrayal. She is sure Grace doesn't know, even now, that there are times when Emma crawls into bed early in the evening, still in her clothes, and just lies there in the dark, engulfed in the silence, her mind torturing her with the memory of Ethan walking out the door. Grace certainly doesn't know how, when the paralyzing memories return, Emma prays for the morning sun to come and pull her out of her nightmares. She couldn't know how hard it is for Emma to get out of bed, never mind function, some days. And Emma is positive Grace is unaware of the time she was found hyperventilating a block from her house—someone called 911, then an ambulance appeared with its siren blaring and lights flashing. She must be unaware of how Emma was terrified and embarrassed at the same time. The weight of her divorce still lingers, but she perseveres, determined to leave that painful chapter behind and embrace whatever the future holds. Some days are better than others.

Grace may not know the specific details of these things, but I swear she can see right through me.

Emma peels off her red rubber gloves and turns to face Grace.

"I'm better, not bitter. And what would you know about how long a person can be 'bitter,' as you call it? You're married, with a great husband, a sweet kid—oh, and a dog. You live in the suburbs of Greenwich, Connecticut, with a white picket fence." She hopes her tone doesn't betray the sadness she experiences most days.

"You know I don't have a white picket fence. I'm sorry. You're right, I don't know what that feels like. But I think I can say with some certainty that you know you can't keep on like this. I see you disappear little by little after these wedding gigs. You can't simply swap a vowel, an E for an I, and be better. As your friend, I truly believe it's time you do something to help yourself."

"You're right. You're always right. Maybe I should move in with my therapist—I'm sure her family would love that," Emma says, grimacing as she puts away the developing chemicals. It's a typical move for her to agree with whatever the other person is saying if only to get out of an uncomfortable conversation. Avoid confrontation at all costs, even if the cost is yourself.

"I'm done in here. Can we look at the upcoming shoots we have booked? Figure out a game plan for the summer and fall? Maybe I can figure out a way to take some time for myself."

Emma sinks into her bed, cozy under her Pottery Barn down-alternative comforter, and mentally plans for tomorrow. She loves Sundays. To her, Sunday is a day to rest, reset, and try to do something nice for herself.

She plans to sleep in and have a leisurely cup of coffee while catching up with the world à la *The New York Times*. Then a good run in Riverside Park, followed by a long hot shower. She may wander around the village, looking for work by an unknown artist to hang in the hall of her condo.

Emma lives in the prestigious Upper West Side of Manhattan. She moved into the two-bedroom condo as soon as her divorce was finalized. Between the sale of their home and a chunk of guilt money from her ex-husband, Ethan, she could afford this top-floor unit in the boutique building designed by architect George Fredrick Pelham. She has Grace to thank for pushing her to jump on this condo when it became available. Grace is friends with the former owners and got Emma a viewing before it officially went on the market.

"Don't think too long about this place. My friends are doing me a favor by showing it to you first," Grace said as she stood fixated on the stunning views of the park and the historic tree-lined block.

Emma wasn't ready to make the leap from her house in the suburbs to a condo in Manhattan, but the impressive ten-foot-high ceilings, expansive windows, and polished hardwood floors were tugging at her dormant artistic side. Her mind was spinning with the possibilities of decorating and making it her own. The Japanese soaking tub and the reassurance of twenty-four-hour security sealed the deal. To this day, she isn't sure which is more important to her—the tub or the security.

But on this Sunday, as Emma wakes with the rain beating against the glass, she questions her desire for the large windows. She closed the thick black-lined curtains last night, but they didn't muffle the sounds of the storm. Emma opens one eye to glance at her Apple watch. *Damn. Only seven o'clock. So much for sleeping in. Okay, I'll meditate, then I can check it off the list. And after my run, I can check exercise off the list.* Meditation and exercise are always on her daily to-do list, but they are rarely checked off. She rearranges her pillows and comforter, leans back, and takes a deep breath.

She begins her mantra—So-Hum. As she breathes in and out, her mind wanders. Her Transcendental Meditation teacher told her this was okay as long as she comes back to her mantra. *So-Hum. What should I do today? The rain has put a kink in my plans. So-Hum. That jerk on Fifth Street really pissed me off yesterday. So-Hum. I should relax—that's what Ethan used to say. "Relax, Emma bear." So-Hum. So-Hum. Breathe in. Breathe out. Ethan—why am I thinking about him?*

"Screw this," Emma says out loud as she flings off the covers and gets out of bed.

She walks barefoot across the polished hardwood floors that lead into her kitchen. The large windows throughout the open-plan living space bring in natural light, creating a feeling of spaciousness. The kitchen was advertised as a chef's dream, with state-of-the-art stainless steel Wolf appliances. Her first purchase for the condo was a microwave and an easy-to-use cappuccino machine. Emma doesn't cook anymore. She remembers how she and Ethan loved to cook together. He would open a bottle of wine on a Friday night, and she would chop veggies for a stir-fry. Ethan would peel the shrimp and mince the garlic. She would set the table. To be closer, they liked to sit side by side at the table rather than opposite each other, enjoying a wonderful dinner and sharing their day. They both had so much to talk about—it seemed they never ran out of things to say to each other. At least, that's what Emma thought.

Emma opens her front door with a cappuccino in hand and sees *The New York Times* waiting for her. She smiles. Tony, the doorman, delivers the paper to her door every Sunday morning. *I wonder if he does this for anyone else.* She sighs as she sits at the small dining table strategically placed for the view overlooking the park.

"God, it's a depressing day," she mutters, opening the paper.

The headline on the front page yells at her in bold black text. "Measles Outbreak Spreads, New York Declares a Health Emergency." She skips that article but makes a mental note—*I should tell Grace about this, but she probably already knows. Grace is on top of everything that could relate to her three-year-old son.* She moves on to page two. "Floods in Iran." "US to Expect Another Bomb Cyclone." "*E. Coli* Found in Ground Meat." The next few pages are as depressing as the first.

She puts the paper down and sips her cappuccino, mindlessly staring out the window. Ethan crosses her mind again. She shakes her head. *Why now? It's been five freaking years since I've seen him.* She picks up the paper again, but her mind keeps wandering, memories bubbling up. Emma Callahan allows them to come…

"Ethan, I'm home. Hey, where are you? You won't believe what happened at today's shoot." She dropped her Coach purse on the hall table, slipped out of her heels, and hung her coat in the hall closet.

"Ethan?"

She found him sitting in their living room, a room they had decorated together. They would sip wine and pore over catalogs of furniture well out of their price range. Their weekends had been spent picking out treasures at flea markets. She thought back to their futile attempt at hanging wallpaper, and the memory brought a slight smile to her face.

"I give up," Ethan had said, standing on the ladder with a sheet of wallpaper sticking to the butt of his jeans.

They'd hired a professional to finish the job. They had transformed the space into a room they loved in and lived in. On winter evenings, they'd light a fire in the faded red-brick fireplace and curl up together on the large gray sectional. Next to the sectional was what they referred to as the "Archie Bunker chair." Ethan didn't ask for much, but he had pushed hard for a recliner.

Emma had stood her ground. She hated recliners. "They take up too much room, and they can't be against a wall because then they won't open."

She'd given in when they found one at Restoration Hardware she could live with. The chair was everything Ethan wanted but more tailored, without the bulk that she hated. They'd ordered one in white along with a matching armchair, which they strategically placed on the other side of the sectional.

This area, with its soft lighting and comfortable seating, was an invitation for conversation and comfort. The place was not a house but a home. Emma and Ethan's home. A home they hoped to fill with kids and dogs.

The kids had never happened, and their dog, Mike, had passed away the year after they moved in.

"Ethan—there you are. What are you doing in the dark?" she asked, turning on the overhead lights. Emma stood for a moment, sensing something was off, but she didn't stop to acknowledge it. Instead, she walked over to where he was slouching in the recliner next to the couch.

"Hey, I was calling for you. Didn't you hear me?" She noticed an almost-empty glass of amber liquid. *Oh my God —he got fired. What the hell will we do? How can we afford to live? I make a decent salary, but we depend on his. What the hell?*

"I heard you," he mumbled.

Is he slurring? "Are you drunk?" she demanded, her tone sharp and accusatory.

"Not yet." Ethan took the last sip of his drink, stood up, and left the room.

"Ethan, what's going on? Where are you going?" She followed him to the kitchen and watched as he filled his glass with scotch, his back to her.

"Want one?" he asked flatly.

Emma hesitated for a split second then said, "Sure. But are you going to tell me why you were sitting in the dark, drinking alone? Ethan, did you get fired? Please tell me you didn't."

Emma shakes her head to rid herself of that memory. She gets up from the table, thinking the same thoughts she has had for the last five years. *Why didn't I say something different? Why did I jump to conclusions? Why didn't I show him I cared? Why didn't I put my arms around Ethan and tell him I loved him? Why didn't I tell him we could make it through anything?*

Emma hates it when these memories return out of the blue. She returns to her bedroom, changes from her pajamas to her running clothes, puts on a jacket, and leaves the condo. Rain or no rain, she needs to run—to escape her memories.

Chapter Three

"This isn't working out the way I was hoping!" – Tigger, Winnie-the-Pooh

Esme

The shrill wail of a siren pierces through her dreams and jolts her awake. Realizing the noise isn't a siren but instead her alarm, Esme rolls over, slams her palm on the clock, and pulls the blanket up to her chin. Prompted by the ungodly hour, the comfort of her bed, and the throbbing in her head, a loud sigh escapes her lips. *I hate this.*

"Time to change thinking this every freaking morning," she mumbles, getting out of her cocoon.

Esme rises at five thirty today, as she has done four days a week for the last one hundred years. Well, that's how it seems to her. Day in and day out, same routine, same old drudgery. But aside from the unreasonable time she needs to get to work, her life isn't as bad as it always seems when the alarm goes off.

In her soft Ugg slippers, she shuffles down the hallway toward the bathroom, taking a quick glance at the closed door of the guest bedroom. Esme senses a tug of annoyance, but it all washes away as she steps into the shower and lets the hot water run down her head, soaking and soothing her. She applies her ridiculously expensive vegan, cruelty-free shampoo to the top of her head, relishing in its luxurious scent, followed by conditioner made for unruly curly hair.

Esme rinses off and steps out of the shower, wrapping a white Egyptian cotton towel around her body. She wipes the fog off the mirror and stares at herself. *I look old, tired, and puffy. I guess that's because I am old and I am tired. When did I become puffy?* She removes the towel and stands naked in front of the full-length mirror. Esme is well aware that she is supposed to embrace her body, thank it for supporting her for thirty-seven years, and appreciate it for carrying a human being for nine months. Instead, she stares critically at herself. *What happened to the girl with a flat stomach, toned thighs, and perfect breasts?* She shakes her head in disgust and turns away from the mirror.

"Time for work," she mumbles.

"Good morning, Anthony." Esme greets her long-time head baker as he skillfully removes the steaming croissants from the oven, filling the bakery with the aroma of their crispy buttery crusts.

He's a short and round man, but what he lacks in stature Anthony makes up for in his sense of humor and warm personality, which shines through his kind eyes and ready smile.

"How was the commute in?" he asks. This is a running joke between Anthony and Esme. She lives above the bakery on Charles Street in the heart of Boston's famous Beacon Hill. She and Cody found the building a year after they were married. Their son, CJ, was born about seven months after the wedding, and they were struggling financially with an infant and one income—Cody's. Their lives took a drastic turn when Esme's father passed away, leaving her with a sizable inheritance. This unexpected windfall enabled them to leave their cramped studio apartment and set up shop in this prestigious part of Boston, complete with an apartment. The apartment has three bedrooms, a large kitchen, two bathrooms, and a living-dining room combo. Cody wanted no part of living above a bakery. This was a battle he couldn't win, and he knew it. She hired Anthony to do the majority of the day-to-day baking downstairs, while she did the creative baking in the apartment. This way, she could keep an eye on the baby and help grow her business. It's a win-win, she would say to anyone who asked how she could juggle it all—career, husband, and baby. It has been this way for years. Prince's Pastries grew from cupcakes, breads, and small pastries to Prince's Pastries and Café, one of the hot spots in the area. Her ambition to succeed drove her to transform the small business into a thriving café, where patrons are met with the enticing fragrances of croissants, muffins, eclairs, and bread straight from the oven and the aromatic scent of coffee beans being roasted. The addition of wedding cakes and catering services led to the need for a full-time team of six to meet the demands of the thriving business.

Esme pours herself a steaming cappuccino and settles in to go over the orders for the day. Even on a Wednesday in April, they are busy. At exactly seven in the morning, Roseanne, Esme's trusted manager, enters through the locked front door. She flips the sign from closed to open and greets Esme with a wide, beaming smile. *Roseanne is in a perpetual good mood. Why aren't I?*

The café buzzes with activity as the regulars begin to arrive—the bankers and lawyers heading to State Street, the young moms and nannies picking up a coffee for themselves and a sweet for the kids before dropping them off at preschool. After the morning rush, Esme returns to the back of the café, behind the big ovens, where she has her quiet place. What was once a cramped, dark storage room, Esme redesigned into an organized and well-lit office. It's here that she doles out the orders. Who bakes what, who delivers, who staffs the front. This is the part of the job Esme doesn't like. She is creative. Esme likes to experiment with flavors and designs. She hates being logical and analytical. Either way, Esme needs to have both the right and left brains working together every day.

Hours later, Anthony pokes his head into the office. "Time to call it a day," he says.

"Jesus, that time already? Have a good night, Anthony. I'll see you in the morning."

She says goodbye to Roseanne, who is closing the shop, and heads up her stairs. Cody is there. Ever since his company downsized and gave up their expensive office space in the city, Cody seems to always be there. As a graphic designer, Cody has unpredictable hours. He often wakes in the middle of the night with a creative flash, which ultimately disturbs Esme. Cody took over the guest room as his office. He removed the bureaus, brought in a desk and drawing table, and left the bed in place. This worked for Cody and, at first, annoyed Esme. *I work in a damn broom closet, and he has an entire bedroom. Which now means no guests.* But Esme adjusted. She always adjusted.

Plus, she knew they never had guests.

"Hi Babe, how was your day? Wine or a cocktail?" he says, giving her a soft and gentle kiss. Esme reciprocates before pulling away to answer him.

"Wine, please. How about a Stags Leap? A good cabernet will taste great on this chilly night." The morning's thought of *time to stop drinking, time to make a change*, goes out of her head when the first sip of Stags Leap settles in the back of her throat.

"I ordered dinner from Legal Seafood. It should be here around six, so we have time to catch each other up on our days."

Esme smiles, sipping her wine.

As if reading her mind, Cody says, "Today was an insane day, and I absolutely didn't have the energy to pull off a Blue Apron meal."

She nods her head, not saying a word until she puts her wine down on the black Carrera marble kitchen island and says, "What made it insane? Did something happen at work?" What she wants to say is, *how hard can it be to stick a Blue Apron meal in the oven?*

Today she had to decorate a small cake with "Happy 24th Anniversary Mom and Dad We Love you Both to the

Moon and Back." Cupcakes surrounded the cake, each with
the name of one of the couple's five kids. Surrounding those
were two dozen cupcakes adorned with sunflowers. Esme
shook her head, thinking of the absurdity of that overly
particular order. She did a cake testing with a prospective
bride and groom with their pain-in-the-neck mothers. Then
orders needed to be placed, the bills paid, and the third
installment for CJ's tuition sent. The thought of CJ pulls
her out of her slippery slide toward *Is this going to be the rest
of my life?*

"I'll tell you what's insane. How expensive CJ's tuition
is. Before you say anything, that's not a dig. We agreed to
this, but it is a bit painful to write that check."

Cody looks down at his phone. "Legal's here," he says as
he gets up, not responding to Esme's mention of the tuition
costs.

She refills their wine glasses and puts place mats, plates,
cloth napkins, and silverware on the kitchen island. They
have a dining room table, but they rarely use it.

"Speaking of CJ," Cody says once they are seated, right
before he takes a bite of his flounder.

Esme looks up, waiting for him to finish. But first, he
has to chew and swallow that large piece of fish he just
shoved into his mouth. *He always does this—speaks and then
fills his mouth up so he can't talk.* "What about CJ?"

Cody sips his wine and says, "He's decided to spend the
summer with his roommate in Kennebunkport."

She looks at her husband, thinking she misunderstood
him. *CJ, not home for the summer? That's crazy.* "What's that

supposed to mean, spending the summer in Kennebunkport?"

"Exactly what it sounds like, Esme. He has an opportunity to spread his wings, and why not? Offers like this don't come around every day." Cody plays dumb, but he must know what's coming.

"That's ridiculous. We've only met Tad's parents once, when we were moving CJ into his dorm room, remember? He is not going the hell up to Kennebunkport, Maine, with total strangers to do God only knows what. He's only nineteen years old. Ridiculous." Pausing to catch her breath, she tilts her head, narrows her eyes, then asks in a low voice, "Why did he tell you and not me?"

Cody puts down his fork and fixes in on his wife. "Because of this—this reaction. CJ knew you wouldn't approve."

"Well, he's right about that. I don't approve. Why do I always have to be the grownup in this relationship? I'll call him after dinner and set him straight. So, is this what made your day so insane we needed to do takeout?"

And there it is. What she has been trying to suppress is now right in front of her, impossible to ignore. Esme can't help but resent her husband for his less demanding job, making her even more envious of the close bond he shares with their son. He had plenty of time to spend with CJ when he was growing up. She spent her time making a name for her business, and if she wasn't working, she was exhausted from working. Cody ignores her dig.

"Call him, but you aren't going to change his mind. Face it, our boy is all grown up. He's in college, and he can pretty much do what he wants. I pray to God that we raised him to make smart choices, but at some point, we need to let him be his own man." He gets up, clears their plates, and throws what remains of their dinners into the trash.

Esme pours herself more wine and says, "I'm going to take a bath."

Esme's bathroom is her sanctuary, her favorite room in the apartment. Some people meditate or do yoga, but Esme soothes her soul in this room. Cody and CJ have always shared a bathroom—the boys' room. This is her space, all hers. From the moment the door swings open over the light-blue-and-white heated tile floor, she's at peace. Esme doesn't know what she likes best about the room. Her go-to retreat includes a 67-inch white cast iron soaking tub, which is perfectly centered under the crystal chandelier that she rescued from her grandparents' home in Wellesley. In the small shower, the cobalt porcelain tiles shimmer under the shower spray, creating the illusion of a deep, tranquil sea. The mahogany vanity, once a dining buffet, also from her grandparents, was restored and repurposed, adding a touch of antique warmth to the otherwise sumptuous room.

She places her wineglass on the bamboo caddy resting across the tub. While the water is running, Esme pours in a capful of her luxurious Lollia bubble bath and lights a lavender candle on the caddy. She sinks into the hot water, letting out a sigh. It doesn't escape Esme that she starts and ends her day with a sigh. Instead of relaxing, Esme is stewing. She can't or won't let go of the conversation with Cody about CJ and his stupid plan to go to Kennebunkport to stay with his roommate and his parents. She takes a sip of wine. *Hold on. Is he staying with Tad's parents, or is he staying somewhere else?*

With her third glass of wine nearly finished, her anger is moving up the scale, no longer a slow simmer but now threatening to boil over. *I'm calling him.*

Esme is well aware this isn't a good idea.

"Siri, call CJ."

"Good morning, Esme." Anthony glances up from the open oven door and smiles at her.

"Morning, Anthony" is all she can manage. She knows she looks like hell; she sure feels like hell, and she is pretty sure she isn't fooling Anthony. *Today is a black coffee day.* She brings the large mug into the office to hide. Esme tries to focus on the list for the day, but she can't let go of last night's conversation with her son. It went from bad to worse. By the time CJ hung up on her, the bath water had gone cold, and all Esme had accomplished was to push him away. He is spending the summer in Kennebunkport, and she could go fuck herself. CJ didn't say that, but that's how Esme feels. Her head is in her hands when Roseanne pokes her head in.

"Hey Esme, are you ok?" she asks softly.

"Oh, good morning, Roseanne. Yes, all good. Is it already time to open? Do you need help out front?" *Please say no. Please say no.*

"I'm opening in a few minutes. I can handle the café

crowd. Tara's coming in at seven thirty, so I think we have it covered."

"Great, and thanks. I'm going to spend some time this morning going over the details for the CBI wedding. Let me know if you need me, though." Esme sips her coffee and sits up straight. *Jesus Christ, I need to get a grip, focus on my business, straighten out my kid, and figure out my life.*

The CBI wedding folder is front and center on her desk. Esme takes another sip of the strong, hot coffee and opens the folder. The contract is on page one.

Armstrong Wedding

- Location—Chatham Beach Inn, Chatham, MA
- Time—9:30 to 6:00
- Guest head count—75
- Welcome mimosa with skewered fresh fruit and mini muffins—9:30 to 10:30
- Ceremony on Ropes Beach—11:00 to 12:00
- Cocktail hour, light passed appetizers and raw bar—12:00 to 1:00
- Sit-down luncheon, family style—poached salmon in dill sauce, grilled spring asparagus, spring peas, Caesar salad, breadbasket—1:00 to 3:30
- Cake-cutting ceremony—4:00
- Live entertainment (photo booth, croquet, bocce ball, and cornhole)—4:00

- New England clam chowder and lobster sliders
—5:00

Page two is the detailed menu listing everything right down to the oyster crackers for the chowder.

With meticulous attention to detail, Esme and her team have curated a menu that is sure to impress both the guests and the bride and groom. They hope this will attract more customers to their catering services.

She puts the folder down. *Do I even want more business?* Between now and the CBI wedding, she has four other weddings, a cocktail party for one hundred at the State House, and a private dinner for fifty at a Beacon Street penthouse. With her elbows on the desk and her head in her hands, Esme wonders if this is all worth it. She has been fighting off a feeling of...well, she doesn't know what it is. She can call it exhaustion, or stress, or anxiety. Esme is emotionally drained.

She pushes back in her pink velvet desk chair and takes a long, deep breath. *I can't do this anymore.*

Chapter Four

"Time doesn't take away from friendship, nor does separation." — Tennessee Williams

Cape Cod is Calling

E llenor, deep in thought trying to conjure her elusive Southern inner child, barely looks up when her cell rings. But her Apple watch makes sure she knows she has a call. She glances at her phone, and a broad grin spreads across her face.

"Hello, Emma."

"Hi, Ellenor."

They both start laughing and talking at once.

"I have Esme on the line. Let me try to conference her in."

"Oh my God, how are you two?" Esme says, her voice bubbling with enthusiasm.

"Esme, it's wonderful to hear your voice. Do I hear your Boston accent getting stronger?"

"Wow, it's been a while since we all talked together. I miss you both so much."

"We miss you, Emma."

"Is everything okay?" asks Esme.

"Living the dream, ladies, living the dream. I have a plan—hear me out," Emma says. "I have the option of staying at the Callahan Cottage at my parents' place for the last few weeks in June. Coincidentally, I have a photo shoot on Martha's Vineyard the weekend before the cottage is available. Who wants to join me and relive our youth?"

"I'm not sure we can survive reliving our youth. I have a catering gig at CBI in June—let me check the dates."

"Ellenor, I checked out your website for your book tour dates. The timing is perfect since your last event is on Nantucket. You can just hop on a plane and come over to the Cape. There's enough room for the three of us at the Cottage."

Esme is back on the phone. "I need to be in Chatham on June 22. The wedding isn't huge, and it's only a one-day event for me. I can come to the cottage earlier, do the walk-through the day before—the wedding is on Saturday—then spend a few days after with you, if that works."

"It works! I'm done with the Vineyard shoot and plan on getting to Orleans the next day. Ell, what about you? Please say you can make it."

Ellenor is lighting a cigarette, contemplating how to answer this very simple question. The thought of "going home" makes her want to curl up on the couch and shut out the world. But these are her people. She can't simply say no and hang up.

"Ell, are you there?"

"Yes, sorry, I'm here. Of course, I can do it. I was

thinking about taking some time off after this tour, so the timing is perfect. Can't wait," she lies.

"I need time off too," declares Esme.

"I need to reinvent myself," Emma responds. "I'll let my family know to get the cottage opened up for us. Ell, you'll need to bring copies of your latest book, signed for Mom and Dad, and Esme, you know my mother loves your chocolate eclairs. These are simple bribes, that's all," she says, laughing as they all say goodbye and hang up.

Ellenor sits on the floor, smoking. *Shit, am I really going to do this?*

Chapter Five

"Embrace uncertainty. Some of the most
beautiful chapters in our lives won't have a
title until much later." — Bob Goff

Emma

E mma hangs up from the call with Ellenor and Emma.
Her mind is whirling. *How the hell am I going to pull
off time away from the studio in June? What was I thinking?*

But the image of the three of them at her parents' Cape
Cod ocean-side cottages fills her with a rush of excitement
and a new energy, despite her concerns. She realizes she gave
the impression that she can free up her schedule and be
available whenever she wants. That's not the case. E&G
Photography has commitments through the fall, possibly
beyond. *I just want to be done, to walk away. If I never see
another bride, it will be too soon for me.* She is sick to death
of smiling and pretending she's as happy as the people who
pose for her. She hates most of them. If they can afford to
hire E&G Photography, they can afford just about
anything. She huffs, shaking her head at the thought of the
money people spend—ten thousand for a baby shower, five

thousand for a gender reveal party. Christenings are less expensive than a two-year-old's birthday party, but not by much.

Years ago, she stopped asking Grace and Dave what they were charging for weddings. Early in their partnership, Grace's husband, Dave, a financial guru, stepped in to manage E&G's finances after noticing some less-than-ideal financial decisions from the two creative partners. Dave has been onboard since, steering their business into financially safe waters and making them a lot of money. He also took over Emma's finances when Ethan left her in a mess. Dave is the person who convinced Ethan to sell the house and give ninety percent of the proceeds to Emma. She has an excellent attorney, but Dave is a friend with incredible guilt-maneuvering techniques. Ethan buckled under Dave's pressure.

Screw it. Grace said I need to do something for myself—I'm doing this. Look out Cape Cod, we're coming home.

Chapter Six

"Not everything that is faced can be changed,
but nothing can be changed until it is faced."
— James Baldwin

Esme

Esme hangs up the phone, smiling as she thinks of how nice it is to have something to look forward to —spending time with her best friends. She is leaning back in her office chair when reality hits. *How can I make this work? Fuck it. I will make it work.*

Lost in thought about the challenges and possibilities of the trip, Esme is jolted back to reality by the sound of Roseanne's voice.

"I locked up, Esme—time to call it a day."

"Good night, Roseanne." She turns off her office light and walks up the flight of stairs to the apartment. The excitement of reuniting with her two best friends has worn off, leaving Esme feeling one hundred years old. She is well aware of her age—forty is beginning to creep around the corner. *The next thing I know, I'll be fifty, wishing for grandchildren.*

She shakes off these thoughts and opens her apartment door. There's Cody, smiling and walking toward her with arms open. It's Friday night, typically date night for them, but the dates are becoming less and less frequent.

"Want to walk to Trivi for a pizza tonight?" Cody asks, mixing their martinis.

Esme closes her eyes, deep exhaustion taking over.

"Honestly, I am dead tired... That's an awful expression," she says, more to herself than to Cody. "Can we get them to deliver? It's still early, so they might not be swamped yet."

"If you want early bird pizza, I'll see what I can do." He leans over to kiss her as he sets her martini down on the glass coffee table. "I'll call them. I'm sure I can get a pizza delivered to the beautiful and famous owner of Prince's."

He grins, and she grimaces.

Esme sets the kitchen island with paper napkins and paper plates. *Mother would be horrified.* Cody opens the steaming box of a mushroom cheese pizza and puts a slice on his plate. Esme's mother, Victoria Prince, would never allow a paper plate or a paper napkin in her home. Never mind eating pizza straight from the box.

"I talked to Ellenor and Emma today," she manages to say between bites, attempting to hide the fact that her mouth is full. Again, she thinks about her mother—her disapproving mother.

"How are the E's?"

"They're both fine." Esme bristles. She has always hated it when other people referred to them by their first initials. In middle school, they were called the Triple E's, after the nasty mosquito-borne illness. The three of them hated that nickname. She remembers when Ellenor punched her oldest brother in the stomach for calling them that. He was furious, but the girls all laughed and ran like hell to get away from him.

"Esme, are you listening to me? I asked how they are?"

"And I said they're fine." She takes a sip of the martini, now warm, before continuing. "We're planning on getting together in June at Callahan's Cottage. You remember that one, right? It's the bigger one, built to look exactly like the main house. I love that place."

She keeps talking before Cody can say anything. "The timing is perfect since I'll be on the Cape anyway for the CBI wedding."

"I thought that was just a day gig, down and back." He says, narrowing his eyes.

"It is, but… I've decided to go down earlier and stay for a while. I didn't take into account that I need to do a walk-through the day before." She takes a large bite of pizza, hoping he won't ask any questions.

"Really? You're going down early and staying? For how long? How long will you be away? How long have you known about this? When were you going to tell me?"

Esme is surprised at his tone, and his questions, and she's too tired to be tactful.

She sighs louder than expected. "Cody, I just told you, I spoke with them today. There's been no plan, no secret, no sneaking behind your back. We decided today." She's acutely aware that this conversation is teetering on the point of no return.

"So you're just telling me now? No discussion, no consideration for me, or for CJ, for that matter." Cody is on fire.

Esme wipes her mouth with her napkin—a stall tactic so that she doesn't slit his throat with the pizza cutter. "Yes, I am telling you now since I clearly just found out. It's hard to tell someone something before knowing about it." She knows that was harsh. *Screw him. The CJ dig is below the belt.*

"I figure if CJ can take off without discussing it with me, I can do the same thing. What's the difference?" *Why is this turning into a fight? What is going on? How did we go from him giving me a kiss to this in a matter of minutes?*

"What about the bakery? Who's gonna run it? How long do you plan to be away? We need to put our heads together and figure this out, Esme."

"Figure what out? The bakery is my concern—my business, not yours. If there is something that needs to be figured out, I'm the one who's doing that, not you." Her voice is raised, and her temper is on speed dial. The cutting words fly out of her mouth, poisoned arrows of unspoken regret and resentment aimed at Cody.

Cody doesn't respond. He runs his hand through his wavy auburn hair. It's getting long and scruffy, just the way Esme likes it, and this is when Cody typically gets it cut. He glares at her, his soft, soulful brown eyes have turned cold and dark.

"Oh, that's right, stupid, stupid me. I forgot the bakery, and that business is all yours. Silly me, I forgot that you're Esme Prince, daughter of Tech giant Andrew Prince, granddaughter of Judge Welsh and his blue-blood wife." Cody takes a moment to breathe. The red flush on his face and his clenched jaw reveal his burning anger.

"I'm going for a walk before one of us says something we can't take back." He pushes back the bar chair, scraping the hardwood floor and avoiding Esme's gaze.

"I think you already did," Esme mumbles, her voice hardly audible as he slams the door. She sits in the quiet apartment, trying to wrap her head around what just happened.

I guess this is a good time as any to get organized. She throws away what is left of the pizza, pours the last of her martini in the sink, and makes a cup of chamomile tea, taking it with her as she goes down the stairs to the back of the bakery. The scent of something baking still hangs in the air, even though the ovens have been turned off for hours. If comfort has a scent, this is Esme's comfort scent—freshly baked bread. She blows on her steaming cup of tea, winces at how hot the first sip is, and pulls out her day-planner notebook. Esme is fastidious when it comes to staying organized. Her planner is full of daily to-dos, each task highlighted in colors representing the importance of deadlines and appointments. Instead of using her planner, Esme writes a list of her immediate tasks on a sheet of paper.

- *check on Mom/house*
- *call accountant*
- *figure out the mortgage on the bakery*
- *confirm tuition for the next 3 years*
- *check in with the financial advisor*

She slips the list into the notebook and puts it away in the top drawer of her desk. Esme climbs the stairs to the apartment, just as she did a few hours ago, and realizes she isn't as tired as she was then. She feels lighter, as if a massive, dense chocolate cake has been lifted from her shoulders.

It's April, it's Sunday, and it's Esme's day to sleep in. It never happens. Internal clocks can be cruel, never letting you forget you are supposed to be up at five thirty.

The sun's bright morning rays flood Esme's bedroom, gently nudging her out of a peaceful sleep. "But it's too early," she murmurs. *Come, my dear, the sun is beckoning. The waves are calling. Come home to the Cape.* Esme's eyes slowly open, the memory of the dream lingering. The warmth of the sand, the smell of the ocean, and a figure standing in the distance, too far to recognize. It leaves her with a peaceful feeling. *Now, that was a wonderful dream.* A contented smile spreads across her face as she yawns and lazily stretches her arms.

Esme has made her bed, cleaned up last night's glasses, downed two cups of coffee, and is going over her to-do list when Cody sheepishly appears in the kitchen. She studies him. His old, well-worn Ralph Lauren flannel pajama bottoms, the faded graphic of a Land Ho T-shirt, his messy bedhead, and the early morning appearance of a five o'clock shadow make him incredibly sexy in her eyes.

"Coffee?" she asks, turning her head away.

"Thanks." He automatically walks toward her to give

her a kiss, the same as every morning—well, every Sunday and Monday morning, when the bakery is closed. The other mornings, Cody is snoring and Esme is working.

Esme accepts the kiss. It's on her cheek, forced and awkward. "I didn't hear you come in last night."

"I tried to be quiet—didn't want to wake you. Thanks," he says, taking the mug of hot coffee out of her hand.

Esme sits across from him at their island and looks directly at him. "I did a lot of thinking after you went for a walk last night." She restrains herself from using air quotes for the word "walk."

He sips his coffee, looking like he wishes he slept in longer.

"Joanne has been bugging me to check on the house. I can do that when I'm on the Cape in June. I think it can wait until then. In the meantime, I'll have Home Watch send me an update."

"Huh?"

Esme stiffens. *Is he listening to me? Does he ever listen to me?* "Joanne would like me to check on the house." She wipes imaginary crumbs off the counter, thinking looking busy will help.

Cody sips his coffee, saying nothing. Esme chews her thumbnail and then just rips the jagged part off.

Again, calmly, she says, "Cody, do you know what I'm talking about? Do you know who Joanne is?"

The tousled hair, the sexy almost beard, the rumpled clothes—all of his sexy appeal goes right out the window when he shakes his head "no."

Esme straightens her shoulders, places the glass of juice

she'd been drinking on the black Carrera marble counter-
top, then—against her own free will—becomes her mother.
She speaks slowly and deliberately to her husband as if he is
an idiot. Not as if he is a child—her mother doesn't know
how to speak to a child, only to idiots.

"Joanne is my mother's nurse—you've met her. She's
been with my mother in Florida for the last four years. The
house she wants me to check on is my mother's house in
Orleans. She wants to reassure my mother that the house is
still standing even though she has Home Watch on a
retainer. Maybe she's thinking of selling it. Maybe I'll sell it.
Does any of this ring a bell, Cody?"

"Yes, of course I know who she is." He shakes his head
as if clearing away the cobwebs. "Is your mother, okay?
Look, I'm sorry about last night." He sips his coffee and,
without looking up, says, "Do you want to do anything
today?"

"I'm going for a run. I'll see you when I get back." Esme
walks toward her bedroom to change, wondering if she and
Cody are merely going through the motions of being a
married couple. They both have chosen not to address the
elephant in the room. Maybe it's because there is a herd of
elephants in the room.

She runs without direction, replaying her life in her
mind—growing up as the rich kid in Orleans, a town of the
haves and the have-nots. She remembers the exhilaration of
running along the shore, enticed by the large rolling waves,
knowing someday she would be out there with them. Her
grandmother is the one who kept a watchful eye on her—
rarely her mother. Esme's grandmother also taught her to

bake, instilling a passion for coloring outside of the lines instead of following the recipe step by step. Her grandmother encouraged her to be creative. *If it fails, it fails. Never be afraid to start over and try again, dear.*

As Esme runs through the Boston Public Garden her thoughts flash to elementary school. Esme, Emma, and Ellenor were inseparable, a team bonded by their love of the ocean and disdain for boys. Things changed in high school —they were still a team, still loved the ocean and everything it represented to them, but boys were no longer the enemy. They all had plans after they graduated from high school. Ellenor was going to move to Baja, California, and write the next Pulitzer Prize-winning novel from the deck of her cottage on the beach. Emma wasn't sure what she wanted other than to marry Ethan and have lots of kids and dogs. Esme planned on spending a year abroad, apprenticing with some of the best bakeries in Paris, Milan, and London. But all that fell apart when she found out she was pregnant.

Esme runs down Newbury Street with the same determination she had when she vowed not to give up on her dreams—nothing and no one could stand in her way. Her run ends in front of the bakery. Perspiring and breathing heavily, Esme bends over with her hands on her knees to catch her breath then looks up at the sign, Prince's Pastries & Café. Dreams do come true. *Be careful what you dream for.*

Chapter Seven

"There is nothing to writing. All you do is sit
down at a typewriter and bleed."
— Ernest Hemingway

Ellenor

Three weeks after the come-to-Cape-Cod call, dressed in
jeans, a Bruce Springsteen T-shirt, black sneakers, and
her ancient brown leather bomber jacket, Ellenor settles into
her first-class flight to West Palm Beach with her little crossbody phone purse tucked into the seat compartment. Maggie's
assistant, Jill, is next to her. Jill has the job of ensuring Ellenor
is always in the right place at the right time and wearing the
right outfit. Jill always handles these aspects of her job with
confidence. The challenge lies in the other part of her assign-
ment—limiting Ellenor's alcohol consumption and discour-
aging strangers from trying to bring her home or vice versa.

Ellenor glances over at Jill, *the girl who will do anything
Maggie asks*. She sighs to herself, thinking about when Jill
came knocking at Ellenor's door three days ago. Ellenor
opened the door, and there was Jill.

"I'm here to help you pack," she said, pushing her tiny, 5-foot-1-inch body past Ellenor.

"Thanks, but I can do it myself," Ellenor said, standing by the open door.

"Ellenor, if you don't let me do my job, Maggie will fire me."

Ellenor didn't think that was true, but just in case, she gave in. *I don't want to be responsible for anyone losing their job.*

She buckles her seat belt, chuckling to herself. Both Maggie and Jill would have a fit if they knew she snuck her "Fuck the Patriarchy" T-shirt into her carry-on bag. *Hmm, maybe I should wear that for the West Palm Beach talk. I'm sure the country club set would love it.*

"Excuse me, I'd like to order a Bloody Mary as soon as you start the bar service. Jill, do you want anything?"

"Thanks, sparkling water for me," she says, pushing her heavy, black-rimmed glasses up on her nose and opening her book, *Atomic Habits: An Easy and Proven Way to Build Good Habits and Break Old Ones.*

"How's the book?"

"I started it yesterday, but so far it's really interesting."

"Have you read *The Subtle Art of Not Giving a Fuck* by Mark Manson? Now, that is a brilliant book."

"Um, no, I haven't." Jill squirms in her seat, trying to tighten her seat belt.

This is going to be a long six weeks. Ellenor squints, looking out the window as the 747 clears the runway and bursts skyward, pushing her back into her seat.

"Ladies and gentlemen, or should I simply say welcome to all people who love to read? I am thrilled to introduce our guest author this evening, and by the size of the crowd, I think it's safe to assume West Palm Beach is as thrilled as I am. As a matter of fact, we sold out in twenty-four hours! Our guest is the best-selling author of ten novels, most recently the award-winning *Where Did the Girls Go?* I have it on good authority that she is working on number eleven. Personally, I can't wait to see what that one is about. I would like to introduce the woman who boldly began her debut novel with the chilling lines,

The storm clouds gathered on the horizon, rolling across the turbulent ocean and becoming dark and angry, but they were no match for the anger brewing in Jolene's icy steel-gray eyes. She knew she could cover up everything and blame it on the storm.

'Burn it down—burn it all down.'

'But we can save the house.'

'Burn it down. Do I need to do it myself? Where's the kerosene?'

Please welcome Ellenor Snow!"

Ellenor takes a quick swig from her Yeti cup, her go-to for concealing vodka. She adjusts her white jacket and walks out on stage with her chin slightly tucked down, looking up through her thick eyelashes. She gazes out at the audience with a coy smile hinting at secrets she might reveal.

"Hello. My name is Ellenor Snow. Thank you for coming out to hear me share my story—actually, my journey—of how I came to stand in front of people who love to read and may have read one of my books. I'm not quite sure how this happened, but here I am."

Ellenor feels a rush of confidence as the audience's laughter and applause fills the room.

"I was born and brought up by the sea in a small town on Cape Cod. If you have been to the Cape, you might understand the vibe, which to me is the magic of its beaches, the secrets hidden in the sand dunes, and the power of the ocean. I've always written—as early on as I can remember. Stories would come to me when I roamed the beaches that were my playground. I wrote a lot about mermaids then. Reading instilled a love for words in me at a young age, and writing seemed to be a natural transition. In high school, I began submitting short stories to contests and won a few. That recognition gave me the courage to keep writing. I left the Cape soon after graduation and moved to Vermont to focus on my writing. I didn't get to where I am today quickly, but every time I type 'the end' I'm shocked that I did it again. Now, that's enough about me. Let me read a chapter for you from *Where Did the Girls Go*."

Chapter Eight

"We all have big changes in our lives that are
more or less a second chance."
— Harrison Ford

Martha's Vineyard

Emma and Grace carefully stow their bags in the overhead bins, taking extra care with their expensive cameras, then settle in for the ninety-minute flight to Martha's Vineyard.

"Honestly, Grace, I don't know why you feel the need to come on this little jaunt. It should be simple. Wealthy famous people eating dinner presented by a Michelin chef, exquisite wines, and, I'm sure, a decadent dessert. I can do this with my eyes closed." Emma buckles her seat belt.

"Those are exactly the reasons I needed to come. I need some dazzle in my life. Maybe I'll pick up some fashion ideas on how the well-put-together woman is dressing these days."

"Sweats all weekend?" Emma asks with a sarcastically sympathetic look.

Grace huffs and gives her a mocking glare, her dark

hazel eyes accentuated by thick black mascara. "Well, no, not sweats. Yoga pants, but those are completely acceptable in Greenwich."

"Lulus are okay, right?" Emma laughs as she puts on her Bose headphones to listen to her favorite playlist—the hits from 2007.

Grace fastens her seatbelt across her Lulu yoga pants then turns to Emma with a smile. "Screw you. I look damn good in these pants."

They are silent for the rest of the flight—they know each other so well there's no need to fill time or space with words.

"Good afternoon, ladies, welcome to the Vineyard. I'm told that you are staying at the Edgartown Inn. Is that correct?" their driver says, loading the luggage into the back of a large black SUV.

"Yes, that's right," Grace says cheerfully. "I'm hungry. Let's check in and find some lunch."

The warm sun beats down on their faces as they sit at an outdoor bistro table, sharing a platter of two dozen oysters and a pitcher of ice-cold beer. Martha's Vineyard is bathed in the beauty of a June day, with the sky, ocean, and salt air all contributing to the stunning scene.

"I swear the air is fresher, and the sky is a different shade of blue here than just about any place I've ever been to, not that I've been to a lot of places. It's so different, but in a seductively peaceful way." Grace sucks down an oyster.

"Everything is different here, including the oysters. Not nearly as good as Wellfleet oysters," Emma says.

"You, my dear, are a Cape Cod snob. This little restaurant is so quaint. How do you know about this place?"

"The Raw Bar is a staple on the Vineyard. I think it's older than you are." Emma's laughter fills the air as she squirts lemon juice onto the oysters.

Grace ignores the age dig, sips her beer, and sits back in the metal chair, looking at her friend across the table. "There's something that I've been wanting to talk to you about, but the timing has never been right. That's the other reason I came along for this photo shoot."

"This sounds serious. Gracie, are you ok?" Concerned, Emma takes off her Ray Bans and looks directly at Grace.

"I'm fine—nobody is dying." She looks up at Emma. "And nobody is pregnant unless it's you."

Emma raises her perfectly manicured hands in denial. "Nope, not me. No chance of that."

"I suppose that's a good thing for both of us." Grace laughs nervously, fingering the gold chain necklace at her throat. "The thing is, Dave got a big promotion. It's an enormous step in his career."

"Wow, I didn't know we gave him a promotion. Congratulations?"

"No, you idiot, his actual job. We are his charity case. Hawkins and Klein offered him a partnership with the firm. It's as a junior partner, but they hinted this is temporary since a senior partner is leaving in the next year. This move will put Dave in place for stepping into the vacant role when the time comes."

"This is great news. Although why do I get the sense there's more to this story?"

Grace folds her paper napkin into a tiny little square and takes a deep breath. "You're right, there's more to the story. There's a transfer tied into this promotion. To London."

"Geeze, that'll be one hell of a commute. How are you guys going to handle this?"

Silence hangs between them for barely an instant before Grace speaks again. This time, her tone is measured, reflecting the weight of her words. "I'm going with him. Me, the baby, the dog, all of us are moving to London."

Emma sits rigid, her face impassive, but inside, she tries to piece together the words she thinks Grace just said.

Grace leans forward in her chair. "Did you hear what I said? He's being transferred to London."

Emma opens her mouth, but no words come out. She shakes her head, frowning, and looks at Grace. "What does that even mean, you're all going to London? Like for good? For real. You're moving away?"

"Yes, I'm sorry, but yes."

Emma is dumbstruck. She can't think of anything to say.

"Are you ok? I'm so sorry to do this, but—"

"Oh, you say you're sorry. You say you're sorry, so that makes this all okay?" she snaps. Her mind is a tornado of confusion, hurt, and anger fighting against each other.

"No, of course not. Please, take some time to digest this news. It took me a while when Dave told me about this, so I've had time to wrap my head around it. I've looked into hiring a temp. That will give you some time to stay on the Cape and think this over. Dave has some ideas about how we can handle the business through this transition that he'd like to discuss with us."

"I can't do this without you, Grace."

Grace puts her hand over Emma's. "We will figure this out. I promise."

Emma pulls her hand away from Grace's, tucks a lock of shiny black hair behind her ears, and sits up straight. "Okay, I guess. It seems like I don't have much of a say in this, anyway. Grace, I need to take a walk—alone."

Before Grace can respond, Emma places her napkin on the table, stands up, and says, "Lunch is on you and Dave." She places her Ray Bans back on and walks away without looking back.

Here we go again, someone else just walking out of my life. Why do people I love find it so easy to leave me? I'll tell you who has never turned their backs on me: Ellenor and Esme. My God, Ellenor and I have known each other since birth, maybe before.

Emma smiles as she walks, remembering the story that she and Ellenor have heard since infancy. Ellen Snow and Betsey Callahan bonded during their pregnancies, discovering they shared the same ob-gyn and had similar due dates. Emma was the first to arrive, and Ellenor was a week behind. The mothers shared newborn challenges, baby clothes, and recipes for homemade organic baby food. Taking the babies to the beach kept them sane, kept them from feeling isolated, even though they had husbands and other children. The stories and memories may change over the years, but one thing that doesn't change is the bond between Ellenor and Emma.

Emma tosses a shell into the harbor, recalling the first day she laid eyes on Esme Prince. The memory is as vivid as if it happened yesterday—a chubby little girl in a ruffled pink one-piece swimsuit, her curls poking out from beneath a pink bathing cap, refusing to be confined. She walked right into the water—the small waves splashed in her face, but she kept walking out toward the bigger waves. An older woman appeared, yelling and waving her arms as she ran toward the girl. Emma's mother sprang into action—she raced into the cold water and snatched the girl up before the oncoming wave could claim her as its own. Emma was enthralled by this girl's boldness, her obvious lack of fear, and best of all, her attitude. Even in a ruffled pink swimsuit, five-year-old Esme Prince possessed an air of sass and spunk. She and her grandmother became part of the beach scene that summer. Ellenor loved Esme as much as Emma did. Their circle was complete. The three E's.

Chapter Nine

"But when alcohol comes in, start running.
Because there's a demon there, and it goes
back to her childhood." – David Gest

Ellenor

Ellenor hears a noise. She's not sure where it's coming from, but it sounds like someone is pounding on her door with a sledgehammer. She winces as she moves the pillows off her head. The sun is shining through her window, adding insult to injury. Ellenor is definitely injured, and the bright sunshine is an insult to her. *I'm still alive—barely. What the fuck is that noise?* Ellenor takes a few minutes to get her bearings. *Okay, I'm in my room at the Nantucket Inn, and I'm alone. All good signs. I feel like I drank a gallon of vodka, or worse, gin—not sure which.* As she struggles to sit up, she takes in the state of the room. Judging by the empty vodka bottle and overflowing ashtray in the nonsmoking room, someone threw quite a party last night. *Ugh.*

The banging continues, and she hears a very faint "Ellenor?" She's confused. *Who's at my door? Who knows I'm here?* The innkeeper would text her for anything she should know, and Jill wouldn't dare knock on her door. Ellenor, unsteady on her feet, slowly makes her way to the door. Her head is throbbing, her mouth full of cotton. As she passes the full-length mirror, she notices she's wearing the same clothes she had on yesterday—black jeans and a long-sleeve button-down denim shirt. The shirt is all wrinkled and buttoned wrong, but she doesn't care.

Ellenor leans against the door, releasing the deadbolt, then unlocks it and opens the door. She inhales deeply. On her exhale, she says in a hoarse voice, "What the fuck?"

Maggie O'Hare is standing in the hall looking as California as California can look. She is a whirlwind of energy as she pushes past Ellenor and barges into the room. "What the fuck? That's what you have to say to me after I fly across this country, which, by the way, is going to hell, and then catch another flight on a God-knows-what kind of airplane that wouldn't accept my luggage? Then I had to walk to this —what do you call it? An inn? I have no clothes, I have no idea where I am, but, my darling, I am here for you."

Maggie stops for a breath, does a quick scan of the room, and puts her hand up to stop Ellenor from speaking. "Okay, before you call security, Jill called me. She said you were in trouble. I am here as a friend, not your agent. Jill and I will get you through these Nantucket commitments and make sure you get to your friends on the Cape as planned. Hopefully sober. I just hope you don't want to slam the door on me once you hear what I have to say."

"Come on in, Maggie."

Chapter Ten

"The past can hurt, but the way I see it you
can either run from it or learn from it."
— Rafiki, The Lion King

Emma

As Emma drives down Route 6A, the familiar sights and smells of the coast bring back memories of her last visit before her world fell apart. She and Ethan stayed in the Callahan Cottage for two weeks in June, the same as what she's doing this year. Only now, there's no Ethan, just Emma. Every spring, her youngest sister emails the family calendar, letting the "kids" know which cottages would be available and when. They each choose what works best for them and their families. Usually, there aren't too many arguments about who gets the best week or the best cottage. She received that email every spring, and for the last five years, she's said, "No thanks. I'm giving up my week."

Soon after their blissful Cape Cod getaway, Emma came home to find Ethan on his way to getting drunk. What she didn't know then was he was looking for courage—liquid courage. She remembers he didn't look her in the eye when he said flatly, "I'm leaving."

"Where are you going?"

"I'm not sure, but I'm leaving."

"Ethan, I'm confused—you're leaving, but you don't know where you're going? What does this even mean?"

He began to move away from her. "I'm leaving you."

Emma remembers those words as if Ethan was in the back seat of the rental car saying them. "I'm leaving you."

And with that, Ethan walked out the front door and out of Emma's life. He left her standing in their beautiful kitchen, leaning against the six-foot butcher-block island, stupefied. Emma doesn't remember how long she stood here. She doesn't remember when Grace and Dave picked her up and brought her to their house. Emma grips the steering wheel tighter as a knot works its way into her right shoulder. She doesn't want to remember any of this, but these memories are relentless when they want to be.

Grace is the one who broke the news to Emma. Ethan had "run away" with the neighbor's Swedish nanny.

"The Mullin's nanny? What's her name, Kerstin, Kristin, something like that?" she asked.

"Her name is Kaisa. She left the Mullins a note saying she was sorry, but there was a family situation, and she needed to leave immediately. They found the note in the morning, after she was gone. They called the agency that Kaisa worked for, concerned about what had happened. The agency got in touch with Kaisa's parents—there was no emergency. Well, as you can imagine, the Mullins were fit to be tied. They both have demanding careers. Who would take care of the twins? Mrs. Mullins tore Kaisa's room apart. She even pushed the mattress off the bed. That's where she found the pictures."

"Pictures?" Emma asked weakly.

"I am so sorry, but Ethan is with Kaisa, wherever that is, and whatever the hell that means."

"That's nuts. She's like nineteen."

"Honey, Mrs. Mullins has the pictures. They're pictures of Ethan and Kaisa together."

"I want to see them." Emma got up and walked to the front door.

The Mullins lived a few houses away from her home—her and Ethan's home. Despite Grace's pleading, she marched down the street and knocked on the Mullins' front door. The meeting was awkward, especially because the first thing Emma said was, "Show me the pictures."

Mrs. Mullins tried to calm Emma down, offering her a cup of tea, or perhaps something stronger.

"Please give me the pictures."

Mrs. Mullins went into the home office and came out with a manilla envelope, which she handed to Emma. "I don't think you should look at these. I am so sorry, dear."

Emma took the envelope in her shaking hand, mumbled thank you, and turned to leave. The last thing she remembers of that day is Mrs. Mullins calling after her as she walked down their flagstone walkway. "Emma, we are going to need those back. It's evidence for us to sue the agency."

Once home, Emma did look at the pictures then threw

up in her perfect bathroom. She lay on the heated marble floor, where Grace found her. That's when Grace called in the reinforcements, Esme and Ellenor.

The *Welcome to Orleans* sign snaps Emma back into the present. As she drives through town, she notices how much has changed in five years. The empty lot next to the library is gone, replaced by a small grocery store. Her favorite clothing store, Head and Foot, is now a trendy designer boutique. But she grins as she drives by the town green and sees the local dive bar is still there with a few cars in the parking lot. After turning down Beach Road toward the ocean, Emma takes a left onto Callahan's Cartway, a private gravel road leading to her family's cottage colony. Her grandparents had the foresight to purchase twenty acres of prime property that ran along the private beach. The property is quintessential Cape Cod at its finest. Her grandparents had built a modest home for themselves and their children, which sits on a high bluff overlooking the ocean. A covered front porch opens into the living room and kitchen, with stunning views of the ocean from almost every window along the back of the house. The large central fireplace, once used to heat the home, is rarely used now. Over time, they added twelve cottages, strategically placing them throughout the sprawling property. Each cottage is named after a different flower, except for the largest one, Callahan's Cottage, which is a smaller version of the main house. This is home base for Emma, Ellenor, and Esme for the foreseeable future.

Emma turns the car onto the shell driveway and pulls

up to Callahan's Cottage. As she steps out and inhales the ocean into her lungs, she releases the memories that plagued her on the drive from the Vineyard ferry.

Chapter Eleven

"Stop worrying about missed opportunities
and start looking for new ones." — I.M

Esme

E sme skillfully navigates her Audi out of the Beacon
Hill parking garage and is greeted by the bright June
sunshine. As she turns right onto Cambridge Street, leaving
the city behind and heading toward Cape Cod, a wave of
freedom washes over her. She selects Dick Dale surf tunes
from her extensive playlist and is transported back in time.

"Esme Prince, you are going to drown one of these
days."

She shook her long caramel-colored curls, the water
droplets scattering and glistening on her tanned face, and
let out a laugh that echoed through the air—a laugh that
exuded pure joy and youthful confidence. "You're just
chicken. If you want me, you know where to find me."

She picked up her surfboard, adjusted her red bikini,
and raced back to the ocean, charging fearlessly into the
surf.

Where has that girl gone?

Esme approaches the Sagamore Bridge, the gateway to Cape Cod. She replaces Dick Dale with Prince's Greatest Hits and takes the Orleans exit straight to Nauset Heights.

Esme's grandparents bought their home in the Nauset Heights neighborhood in Orleans in the late 1940s. The cottage was bare bones. Even so, the judge and his wife would escape to their cottage for the month of July, enjoying a simple way of life. He loved to fish, and she enjoyed spending her days bringing her easel to the bluff to paint the ever-changing landscape of Nauset Beach. Over the years, the simple cottage grew into a charming crafts-man-style home with proper insulation, updated plumbing, and electricity. After Esme's mother, Victoria, was born, the Welshes spent the next few years upgrading the cottage into a year-round home, including dormers, a sleeping porch, a two-car garage, and a full basement. They planned on retiring there, but Victoria's divorce, which left her basically homeless, changed all that. She had a three-year-old daughter, no job, and no intention of ever getting one. Victoria's divorce attorney made it quite clear that her client required a substantial amount of alimony and child support to allow mother and daughter to continue with the lifestyle they were accustomed to. Esme's father, done fighting with Victoria, agreed. Esme's grandparents tore down the wonderful old house and rebuilt it into what was then considered a trophy home, a stark contrast to what it had been. Victoria and five-year-old Esme moved in the summer before Esme began first grade.

As Esme intentionally drives past her childhood home,

she lowers the music and slows the Audi. She takes a left, then a right, and pulls up in front of 51 Nauset Road. Without a truck in the driveway, she finds solace sitting in front of the house, admiring the changes he has made to the old cottage, wondering about the endless possibilities, all the what-ifs.

Chapter Twelve

*"The most beautiful discovery true friends
make is that they can grow separately
without growing apart." – Elisabeth Foley*

Reunited

"Oh my God, you're here!" Emma shrieks, jumping off the front porch. She pulls Esme out of the car and into a bear hug, whispering, "I've missed you." She takes a step back and exclaims, "Look at this car—a convertible, no less. Esme, you're driving a little red Corvette. When did you get this? It's so you."

"It's an Audi, not a Corvette. Cody drives the sensible car."

"Oh, and here I was thinking you were in your Prince era again. I half expected to see a raspberry beret on top of those curls of yours."

The friends laugh at the memory of Esme's infatuation with Prince and her elaborate schemes to become his backup dancer.

"Shut up. While you and Ellenor were mooning over Boyz II Men, I was digging Prince, thanks to her brothers playing his music non-stop. Prince was so much cooler than your silly little boy band." Esme smiles and hugs Emma again. "I have so missed you and your uncoolness."

Emma huffs. "I don't think so. You wanted to marry Prince so your name would be Esme Prince Prince. You were the uncool one." She laughs as she reaches into the trunk for the luggage. "Let me help you with your bags. Geez, you have a lot of stuff."

"I stopped at Nauset Provisions for a few things. If nothing else, we will eat and drink well."

"Oh, I'm sure we will do more than eat and drink. Ell texted—she should be here soon. She flew in from Nantucket and is picking up a car at the Hyannis airport. Come in and pick out which bedroom you want. I've already laid claim to mine."

"Of course you have." Esme pulls her Louis Vuitton carry-on bag out of the front seat and wraps her arm around Emma's waist. "Not much has changed, has it?" she says as they approach the front porch of Callahan's Cottage. She stops for a minute to take in what she remembers as her home away from home. The shingles are more weathered than she remembers, and the white trim has faded from the sun and salt air. Time appears to stand still on the front porch, with the same rocking chairs and wicker furniture from her youth. She smiles, a subtle warmth spreading through her like a comforting hug. *When was the last time I felt at peace with myself?*

Probably the last time I was here.

Esme picks the bedroom across from Emma's. She puts her luggage on the bed and lies back on the patchwork quilt. She feels the cool, clean air from the open window drift gently over her. A lifetime of memories, the sound of the seagulls, and the peace of this place wash over Esme, saturating her entire body. She takes deep, cleansing breath, but her moment of Zen is broken by the honking of a horn and blaring music. Instead of being annoyed, she's thrilled —Ellenor has arrived.

Emma and Esme are hardly out the door when Ellenor jumps out from behind the steering wheel of her rental. They are ecstatic, talking over each other, laughing to the point of tears.

"These are tears of joy," Emma says, pointing to each of them. "God, Ell, I thought Esme had a lot of luggage. How many suitcases did you bring?"

"Yeah, I've got a lot, but remember, I've been on tour for six weeks. What's Esme's excuse?" she says jokingly, pulling a black Michael Kors weekender bag out of the trunk. "At some point, I'm going to need to do laundry. But first things first—what's on the agenda? Where the hell do we start?"

"We start with a bottle of chardonnay on the porch. Emma, you and Ell bring all this stuff to her room. I'll get the wine and meet you there. Oh, and Ellenor? The washing machine is where it's always been."

"She's still bossy. Some things never change," Ellenor mouths to Emma, smiling.

Chapter Thirteen

"We didn't even realize we were making memories; we just knew we were having fun."
— Winnie-the-Pooh

Wednesday

"Cheers to us for making this happen. Never underestimate the power of us—when we set our minds to it, there's almost nothing we can't do," Ellenor says as she stands with her glass raised.

"Cheers to us"—Esme raises her glass as well—"My God, when was the last time we all were together?"

"When you both came to save me." Emma's words slice through the cheers like a machete, shredding their joy.

Emma, Ellenor, and Esme haven't seen each other in five years. It was Ellenor and Esme who dropped everything when they got the call from Grace—Emma was in trouble. She needed her best friends. Esme and Ellenor got to her house as soon as they could, shocked to see the state of the house and of Emma. They hugged, kissed, and cried while cursing every man on the planet. They pulled her up off of the proverbial floor of broken hearts, covered in shards of glass. They thought Emma would "take to her bed," that they could bring her tea and dry toast every few hours.

"She's sick, and she needs to rest, like when a person has the flu or consumption," Ellenor said.

But Emma wasn't sick. She didn't lay in bed like a model patient. She walked around the house in a state of agitation, sometimes breaking things. One minute she was talking about getting organized and preparing the house to sell, and the next minute she was on the floor, hugging her knees in tears.

Ellenor pulls Emma in for a hug. "I'm sorry it's been so long." Then, in true Ellenor fashion, she adds a positive spin. "Remember what Marilyn Monroe said."

"Happy birthday, Mr. President?"

Ellenor shakes her head in mocked disgust. "No, silly. She said, 'Be with a guy who ruins your lipstick, not your mascara.'"

"Well, that hasn't happened yet. Not sure it ever will. But while I'm waiting for that to happen, why don't we stay in tonight and yack, drink, eat, repeat?"

"Sounds like a wonderful plan."

"I think it's a smart move—for our safety and reputations," Esme says, pulling food out of the refrigerator for a charcuterie board.

"What reputations?" Ellenor laughs, then checks to be sure they are fully stocked with wine.

The three friends settle in on the small side porch of the cottage, taking a minute to savor the vast brilliance of the ocean below them.

"This never gets old. Thank you, Emma, for bringing us

together. I need it. I need you guys," Ellenor says, leaning back in the old white wicker rocking chair.

"Sounds like you need to go first, Ellenor. What's going on?"

"I have writer's block."

"You always say that when you're starting a new book."

"No, Esme, I think it's different this time. My contract has had me pumping out a book a year for the last five years. That doesn't include the books I wrote before they picked me up. This is the last year, and I think I'm empty. I don't think I have any more stories to tell. The proverbial well has run dry."

"That's a lot, five books in five years. Who can do that? Who can do that and write something that's quality, not just fluff?"

"Lots of people. You would be amazed at how prolific some best-selling authors are.

Think of your favorite books and research how many books that the author has written. I think you'd be amazed at just how many successful books they've published."

"You're my favorite author. And you are also a best-selling author," Emma says encouragingly.

Esme is sitting on the other wicker rocker, feet curled up under her, wine glass in hand. She's quiet, listening to her friends talk. Then, in one abrupt movement, Esme bolts up straight and sets her wineglass on the white wicker side table. "Write about us," she loudly declares.

Ellenor and Emma lock eyes with Esme, their brows furrowing in confusion as they simultaneously ask, "What did you just say?"

"I said, write about us. Tell our story about growing up on the Cape. We have such awesome memories, unbelievable times. I wonder how we survived some of the messes we got ourselves into."

"Frankly, I'm fairly sure that my guardian angel is regretting her decision to stick with me," Ellenor says with a laugh.

"I'm serious about this. Ell, think about it. You can recreate our magical childhood."

Remember the summer when we were mermaids? I remember Mrs. C standing at the shore, telling us to get out of the water. We'd yell back, 'We can't walk on land—we're mermaids!' And she'd yell louder, 'Get out of the water now!' And Ell, you would roll into the beach, legs squeezed together, like a mermaid. Emma and I would drag you up the beach, telling Mrs. C she was killing you. Write about us sleeping on the beach. How many young girls get to sleep under the stars on Nauset Beach? Being at your house was one of my favorite places."

"My house? My house was a dump. You want me to write about how poor we were?

Write about the lobster traps piled high in the front yard? Should I add in all the boats behind the house—some working, most not? Oh, I can mention the cars. All my brothers' cars in their various states of disrepair. Do you think I should mention the old buoys scattered around, and how we had to be careful not to trip on a random anchor? You are crazy, Esme. Stick to baking."

"Your house was not a dump. I loved being there. To me, it was magical. Your parents always let us do what we wanted as long as we came home in one piece. I remember your mother saying to us, 'Have fun, stay safe, and come home in one piece.' We were planning on watching the full moon rise over the ocean and then camping out on the beach. Remember how we gathered driftwood for our fire and packed our backpacks with all the junk food we could manage?" Esme said, her words carrying a touch of wistfulness.

"I remember that," Emma chimes in. As she shifts in her chair, it's evident that Emma is fully focused on listening to their shared memories. "Esme, you brought the junk food. You always had the best. I snuck three sleeping bags out of the house, praying my parents didn't catch me. They would have grilled me about why I was bringing sleeping bags to a sleepover at your house," she says, looking at Ellenor.

"I think it's a fabulous idea. Simply change the names of the guilty girls. That would be a good name for the title, *Guilty Girls*." Esme throws back her head, sending peals of unrestrained laughter across the bluff.

Ellenor is quiet, listening to her friends talk excitedly about what she should do. She can't count all the times she has heard "You should write a book about so and so. It'll be great. And you can credit me for the idea when you accept your Oscar." Her thoughts are churning, ideas slowly bubbling up to the surface. *Esme may be onto something.*

"Ell, are you listening to us? Come on, think about this, seriously. We had an amazing time growing up here. Remember riding Mr. Crockett's horses on the beach? Esme's took her for an unexpected swim, yours decided to roll, sending you jumping off just in time before getting crushed. And mine just did what she wanted. I remember Ethan saying we all had a death wish, doing that, riding bareback on the beach. He said we weighed about as much as a postage stamp compared to those horses." Emma's eyes soften, hinting that these memories are bittersweet for her.

"*When We Were Mermaids*," Ellenor whispers, her voice barely audible above the roar of the surf below.

"What?"

"The title can be *When We Were Mermaids.*"

"I like it." Esme raises her glass in approval.

"I'll give this some thought. Sounds more realistic than me pretending I'm Southern. Who wants more wine?" asks Ellenor, heading toward the kitchen door. She wants the focus of this conversation to turn to somebody else.

Emma quietly sinks into memories that have been buried for years. Riding horses bareback on the beach, skinny dipping in the ocean, the joy of young freedom. *Ethan.*

Ethan Harrison was a summer kid. His parents owned a large home in the Nauset Heights neighborhood with million-dollar views of Nauset Beach. He would arrive as soon as his private school ended mid-May and return home on Labor Day. Ethan and a small group of other summer kids fit in with most of the locals, which included Emma, Esme, and Ellenor. For the most part, they all had very little parental supervision. Their days were spent surfing, boogie boarding, working on their tans, unaware of how fortunate they were to be young with the ocean as their playground. Ethan and Emma moved from the friend stage the summer before their freshman year in high school. When they were younger, they were often mistaken for brother and sister. Both had striking blue eyes, Ethan's the color of the ocean, Emma's a deep shade of violet. Their jet-black hair was pin-straight. Emma's was long, well past her shoulders, and Ethan was always pushing his hair out of his eyes. They were tall and tan, thin and fit.

"Emma, more wine?"

She looks up to see Ellenor standing in front of her, tilting her head.

"You okay?" she asks.

Emma straightens her shoulders and tucks her hair behind her ears, catching one of her large gold hoop earrings in the process. "Yes, thanks."

"Where were you? Deep in thought?" Ellenor asks, filling Emma's glass. The glasses at the Callahan Cottage are anything but fancy. Most are recycled mason jars, easily replaced if needed.

"Oh, I was just daydreaming, smelling the salt air, listening to the waves. It's so peaceful here."

Ellenor fills Esme's glass and sits back down in the large wicker rocker. She's quiet for a minute, then says, "Emma, it's your turn with the talking stick."

Esme perks up. "You still have that?"

With a smug smile and a wiggle of her thick eyebrows, Ellenor produces the talking stick she'd hidden under the pillow on the rocker. "I sure do!"

The talking stick—a piece of their childhood. The three

of them crafted it one evening during a full moon, sitting on the beach in front of Ellenor's house. Emma found a perfect piece of driftwood, bleached to a soft gray by the sun and the salt water. The stick was about a foot long with a wavy grain and knots and bumps. They wrapped it in different colored yarns and added a seagull feather. Over the summer, they added shells and small beads until they were sure it was perfect. The talking stick became a symbol of their youth. They made it in a time of innocence, when they believed in magic and miracles, when they believed they were invincible.

"I can't believe you still have this. I love that you brought it," Emma says. "But I'm not ready to talk."

Esme gets up and takes the talking stick out of Ellenor's hand. "Give me that. I am ready to talk," she says defiantly. "My son hates me. I think my husband is sick of me. I think I might be sick of him. I'm exhausted. The bakery is killing me, and the catering business is adding nails to my coffin." Esme sits back down and glares at her friends as if daring them to disagree with her.

"That's a lot to unpack, Esme. Where do you want to start? How about why you think CJ hates you?" Ellenor asks.

"I'm sure you both think I'm being absurd, but it's all true. He hates me because he would prefer to be in Kennebunkport for the summer instead of coming home to me, his mother. Why would he want to be with his college roommate, somebody he's with all the time? Oh my God, do you think he's gay?"

"So what if he's gay? I know you don't care about that. What's really eating at you?" Emma asks.

Esme draws in a breath before saying, "No, I don't think he's gay, and you're right, I really wouldn't care. You guys know that. But I want him to experience what I had growing up— this place is so special. I was so busy working that I barely had time to bring CJ to the Cape when he was little. I'd try to get down here as much as possible on my days off. But I let my business take precedence, and now I'm paying for it. I thought he'd just naturally gravitate to the ocean. Salt-water is in his veins. This is the only place in the world I want to be. I want him to have what I had, what we had." She sits back in the rocker, quiet, tapping her hand on her heart.

"Why wouldn't you want to be here? We all do. Look at what we had—have." Emma gestures toward the water, a mesmerizing blend of different shades of blue, the waves washing onto the Callahan's sandy white beach. The sun is dipping into the horizon, adding a soft glow to the picture Mother Nature is painting for them.

"Esme," Emma continues gently, "CJ is spreading his wings. No offense, but I wouldn't want to spend my summer in Boston with my parents. Your apartment is beautiful, but probably not where a college kid wants to be. Kennebunkport has the beaches, the ocean, and the summer vibe. Not as cool as the Cape's, but still." She laughs. "I think you should be proud that you've instilled a love of the ocean in your son. Now, if he was spending the summer in the desert, I would be concerned. Have you thought about offering him your mother's house? Maybe suggest he and his friend switch beaches up, spend some time here before he goes back to school."

"Yeah, like my mother would ever consider letting him use her house. She was a bitch to me when I'd bring him down the few times I did." Esme huffs.

"Alright then, next on your list—Cody."

Esme sips her wine, shrugs her shoulders, and says, "Cody. I don't know, I think we're in a rut." She stops herself, seeming to weigh her next words before she speaks. "I'm jealous, resentful, whatever you want to call it, because I'm the one who gets up at five thirty in the morning, four goddamn days a week. I'm the one that has to go to work while he gets to sleep in. His work has always been flexible, but now that he works from home permanently, I want to murder him. He gets up when he wants, probably has a leisurely cup of coffee, and if the mood strikes him, he goes to the gym. *Then*, when he is all done focusing on himself, he spends a few hours drawing his stupid cartoons."

"Those cartoons aren't stupid, Esme, and Cody is extremely talented," Ellenor says. "He's a visual artist, an illustrator. Honestly, if I ever write a kids' book, I want Cody to illustrate it. So, what else you got—and when did I become the one offering advice?"

"He's always there, at the apartment. I leave in the morning, he's there. I come home in the afternoon, he's there. I am never alone. And you might not know this, but I value your advice—most of the time," Esme says with a hint of sarcasm.

"Is the house a mess when you come home? Are you the one that always makes dinner?"

"No Ell, he cleans up, and he's in charge of dinner. But sometimes it's takeout. I'm just tired, you guys. Tired of the same old routine, tired of fighting with my kid. I'm tired of Cody. That's all—it's nothing, really."

"Oh well, if that's all, then I'm tired too," Ellenor says sarcastically. "But seriously, you guys, it's almost midnight and I'm exhausted. This tour has almost killed me. I need to go to bed, but we aren't done with putting Esme back together again. From Humpty Dumpty, in case you're wondering."

"Not a bad idea. Tomorrow is going to be a long day. Do you both know what you are bringing tomorrow?"

"Yes, Esme," Ellenor says.

"How many summer solstices have we survived?"

"Not enough, Emma. I pray we have hundreds more to look forward to." Esme stands.

"I'll be happy with thirty more solstices," Ellenor says. "Good night, Esme. Good night, Emma."

"Good night, moon," they chimed together.

Chapter Fourteen

"Summer is always the best of what might be." – Charles Bowden

Summer Solstice

The sun has been up since five o'clock, and Esme isn't far behind. *This is a cruel joke from Mother Nature—I get up this time every freaking day. But today is different. It's the Solstice.* With a yawn and a stretch, she cheerfully throws off the covers and starts her day.

Once Esme has brewed a pot of coffee, she gets to work putting together their breakfast and lunches, along with enough food to feed all the fishermen in Orleans.

The wicker basket filled with paper products, cups, tablecloths, and plasticware is jammed into the back of the Jeep, along with beach chairs, wind screens, boogie boards, and the required shovel, tow rope, and tire gauge. An oversized beach bag, crammed with towels, beach blankets, sunscreen, and extra hats, is shoved onto the floor of the back seat. And now she is standing in the driveway, looking at her watch and considering honking the horn when Emma appears with a large Igloo cooler from the garage and two faded navy blue striped beach bags.

Esme grabs one. "Do you have—"

"Yes, I have wine, beer, Prosecco, tequila, OJ, and water," Emma says. "Also a corkscrew, beer opener, and Advil. Where's Ell?"

"Oh, I don't know, sleeping? By the time we get going, it's going to be the winter solstice."

"Here I am. Sorry, I'm still on San Francisco time. Jesus, Esme, how do you get up this early every morning? And before you ask, I have packed my portion for this Summer Solstice. The talking stick, music, Sun In, trashy magazines, and Scrabble. I stopped in town yesterday, picking up a few things, but when I got home, I found the old Scrabble game right where it always was, in the living room. I don't know why I'm bringing the last two, we never read or play Scrabble on the beach," she says, her voice scarcely above a whisper, still groggy from sleep.

Esme stands back and takes in her friends, these two women whom she loves more than almost everyone else she knows. *What the hell are they wearing?*

Emma has jammed her hair under an old faded red Orleans Cardinals baseball cap. Esme can't help but feel a pang of envy as she admires her friend's long, muscular legs in the faded cut-off jeans, wondering where on earth she found those pink Uggs. But it's the well-worn white oxford shirt with the monogram E that has Esme questioning. *E for Emma, or E for Ethan?* Ellenor's face is hidden beneath a large army-green wide-brimmed hat—but it's not the hat that has Esme staring, it's the cat-motif pajama top and the plaid pajama bottoms.

"God, you look like Christmas morning gone bad," Esme says teasingly, taking a bag from Ellenor.

"Well, little miss perfect, just wait until you get melanoma on your beautiful face, and you'll be dressing like this."

"Don't think so," Esme mutters, cramming into the back seat. Ellenor rides shotgun, and Emma is in the driver's seat, adjusting the rearview mirror.

"Do you remember how to drive on the beach? Don't forget you need to put it in four-wheel drive. I put the tire pressure down to 15, but maybe we should double-check it."

Mr. C—Emma's father—purchased the brand-new 1990 Jeep Grand Wagoneer, intending to use it for many years. He cherished this car, his pride and joy, but as his daughters moved from wonderful children to teenagers, he somehow lost his rights to the car. Katherine, the oldest daughter, was the first to sneak out of the house late at night with the Jeep as her escape plan. She then taught her sister Eileen how to put the car into neutral and roll it silently out of the driveway to not wake their parents, and Eileen, in turn, taught Emma. None of the Callahan sisters had driver's licenses when they began that summer ritual. At least Maureen, the youngest, waited until she had her license to follow in her sisters' footsteps. By that time, the Jeep had gone from the family car to the beach buggy. Mr. Callahan would wash and wax it every Labor Day and put it into the garage for the winter. He would start it up the week before Memorial Day, checking the battery, tires, and fluids to be sure it was ready for the summer.

"Esme, we are fine. I've been driving on the beach since before I was supposed to be driving on the beach."

"But it's been years since you drove on the beach. It changes every day, sometimes hourly. We have no idea of what to expect. Tell you what, I'll be nervous for all of us," Esme says from the back seat.

"Relax—we've done this a hundred times. I'm a Callahan, remember?" Emma puts the Jeep in drive and steps on the gas, driving across her parents' front lawn.

The three friends are silent as Emma grips the wood steering wheel, focusing on keeping the Jeep upright and maneuvering over the bumpy dirt road toward their childhood haven, the Atlantic Ocean.

The dirt road ends at the top of a small hill overlooking the splendor of the ocean and the miles of wide-open beach. Emma stops, as they have always done at this spot. This spot, this moment in time, never, ever ceases to amaze Esme and her friends. It's as if Amphitrite, the sea goddess, is inviting them to her personal paradise, creating a sense of harmony in their world.

Emma lets out a deep cleansing breath, puts the Jeep into four-wheel drive, and slowly steers it down the narrow sandy path, just wide enough for one vehicle, leading down to the beach.

As if on autopilot, she automatically turns north and skillfully drives along the shoreline to the farthest accessible point. Beyond that is protected land—no vehicles, no bikes, no horses. To the left are the sand dunes protecting the homes on the bluff. To the right is nothing but white sand and the sparkling Atlantic Ocean. Even at this time of the morning, there are already a few trucks parked, chairs and coolers set up for a long day on the beach, fishermen who have been here since dawn, and a group of young moms with their toddlers. The throngs of summer residents haven't arrived yet, but they will be here soon enough.

She parks the Jeep on the sand, and they sit there for a moment, silently appreciating the incredible beauty around them. With an unspoken understanding, they exit the Jeep and walk to the water's edge to test the temperature. The tide is low, and the waves are friendly—perfect for swimming.

"Damn, that's cold," Esme says, breaking the spell and running back to the Jeep.

"When did you become a wimp? Try swimming in the West Coast water," Ellenor says.

They unpack the Jeep in what might be considered organized chaos. Beach chairs are pulled out of the back and tossed on the sand. Next are the coolers, umbrellas, and beach bags, and last to come out are the windscreens. Mrs. Callahan made these canvas screens years ago when a particular renter complained that the beach was too windy, which made the sand blow and, in turn, ruined their family's vacation. She spent that winter sewing large pieces of canvas together to create the screens, which are about four feet high and twenty feet long. Mr. Callahan made wooden dowels that fit into pockets strategically sewn into the canvas. His instruction to the renters is always, "Slip the dowel into the slot and hammer it into the sand with a good mallet." He also supplies the mallet.

For Emma, Esme, and Ellenor, the windscreens are more for privacy than wind. They place one on each side of the Jeep, parked horizontally to the ocean, to obscure them from anyone walking by. Just the way they like it. Just the three of them, no interlopers.

"Who wants a mimosa?" Ellenor asks, opening up the cooler that will be their bar for the day. She has three red solo cups lined up on the small beach table, ready to go.

Two hands are raised, and Ellenor masterfully opens the bottle of Prosecco, pours equal amounts over ice, and scarcely skims the top with orange juice. Not bad for eight in the morning.

"Let's play, 'What Would You Do If You Could Do Anything?'" Ellenor says, curled up in her beach chair, both hands wrapped around the solo cup.

Emma starts. "I'd declare world peace, and people would listen to me."

Esme and Ellenor glance at each other and then at Emma.

"Let's start out small—something that might be achievable," Esme says, smirking.

"Okay, Esme, since you're changing the rules, you go first."

"Leave Cody?"

The beach becomes strangely quiet, as if someone pressed the mute button on all the surrounding noise. The seagulls stop squawking; the waves stop crashing to the shore, and Ellenor and Emma stare at their friend astonished, speechless.

Finally, Ellenor breaks the silence. "What are you talking about? Last night, you said you were in a rut. Why on earth would you say you want to leave him? Esme Prince, it's too damn early for this bombshell, and I'm not even close to awake enough to process it in my brain."

Esme wants to grab those words and shove them back into the personal interior closet deep inside her mind. This closet is where she puts anything she wants to forget, and she keeps the door shut. But these are her best friends, her sisters—better than sisters. They are her tribe. *If I can't tell them, who can I tell?*

Emma finishes her drink in two large gulps. "Esme and Cody breaking up? How can that be? If you can't make a marriage work, who can? I'm undoubtedly the last one that should offer marital advice, but Cody is a good guy. He loves you. You've been together since you were in high school. My God, how many years is that?"

"Too many, and that's the point. Yes, I know he's a good guy, but I'm bored—he's boring. My life is a mundane routine. There has to be more than this." She takes the last sip of her drink and says, "He is the only person I've had sex with in the last twenty years. And that has been less and less frequent. There, I said it. Go ahead now and start with your laughing and stupid jokes."

"Seriously? Only Cody, for all this time?"

Emma glares at Ellenor. "Esme, we would never be so callous as to make fun of something so important to you.

It's just a surprise—a big surprise. We thought you were the perfect couple. At least, I thought that."

"I'm sorry, but as Emma said, this is a huge surprise. Have you met someone? Ya know, random sex isn't all that it's cracked up to be. It can be embarrassing, messy, dangerous—it's really something that should be avoided at all costs."

Now Emma and Esme turn to stare at their friend.

"And you would know about this how?" Esme asks.

Ellenor manages to get out of her beach chair with some dignity as she says. "Oh no, don't try to turn this toward me, Esme Prince. You started it, and we are going to try to figure this out. And we will, or we will die trying. Who wants another drink?"

Armed with her second mimosa of the morning, Esme loosens up. "You guys know the story. Cody and I never had a chance to be a couple just getting to know each other, having fun. I'm ashamed to say it was pretty early in our relationship when I found out I was pregnant. I'm not sure we would have stayed together if it wasn't for that. But we did what our parents wanted us to do, and that was to get married as quickly as possible. For my mother, it was to save face, and for Cody's parents, it was the right thing to do. And then after the wedding, the focus was on having the baby, not on us as newlyweds. The pressure was insurmountable. How would Cody finish college? What was I supposed to do? Where would we live? How would we live? I don't think I shared any of this with you guys. Honestly, I was embarrassed. I felt like I had royally screwed up and let everyone down. Thank God my grandparents stepped in to help us."

"That was almost twenty years ago. There must be some wonderful memories, good times when it was just the two of you?" Emma asks.

"But that's the point, it was never just the two of us. In the beginning, my grandmother was always hovering over me. Then CJ was born, so we were never alone, and it seems like now that we are alone, we're strangers. I still find him attractive, but it actually pisses me off that he's aging so well and I'm not. When CJ was younger, we would argue about stuff. We would fight because we cared, if that makes sense. But as the years passed, I think we just stopped caring. There's no passion, no reason to love or to fight. And once CJ left, the routine became monotonous, like I said last night. The most emotion I've seen out of Cody in years was when I told him I was coming here to spend time with you guys. But I think it was more that his nose was out of joint that I didn't consult with him first. The bottom line is, neither one of us cares enough to fight. I can't imagine going through the rest of my life like this. That's why I think it might be nice to put myself back out there. Ya know, test the waters."

As if on cue, a tall, muscular man, clad only in swim trunks and earbuds, comes jogging down the beach, seemingly lost in his run. As he gets closer, the three women sitting side by side in their chairs turn their heads in sync to watch him pass.

Esme gets up from her beach chair saying, "Like him. I

could test the waters with him. I'm tired of talking. Who wants breakfast?"

They snack on hard-boiled eggs, homemade granola, and fruit cups, discussing the pitfalls of relationships, dating, not dating, divorce, solid marriages, Esme's marriage, and whatever else they can think of to toss out for the wind to solve the issue of love. Emma's declaration of solving world peace seems easier.

Emma strolls to the water's edge to rinse off her hands. She stands alone, staring out at the ocean. Her heart is heavy—the morning's conversation stirred up bitter memories of her divorce. *I knew it would be a mistake coming here.* She turns to walk back to her chair.

"Emma Callahan? Is that you?" It's the handsome jogger standing in front of her, smiling, head tilted.

She's taken aback. *Who is this guy? Damn, he's hot.* "Yes, I'm Emma Callahan," she says hesitantly.

"Sorry, I'm sure you don't remember me. I was the best man at the Maloney wedding. I'm Ben Maloney," he says, putting out his hand.

Emma shook his hand, completely confused. "The Maloney wedding?"

"Yeah, Megan and Bill Maloney. Bill's my brother. You were the photographer." He is clearly trying to jog her memory. "It was in April, Tavern on the Green. Cold, crappy day. You were great, so patient with us, who were already doing pre-ceremony shots."

"Ah yes, sorry. I have to admit, I don't remember names, but I remember the weddings. So, hello then. What are you doing on my beach?" She smiles, surprised at her little flirtation.

He flirts right back. "Oh wow, you own this whole beach? Impressive. I'm here with some friends for another wedding. It seems like that's all I do—always the grooms-man, never the groom."

She laughs. "I think it's always the bridesmaid, never the bride."

"I say it's equal opportunity of coming in second. But what are you doing here, besides surveying your beautiful beach?"

God, he's got an incredible smile and a body to match. "This is where I grew up, so I'm back to my roots for a while this summer. I've missed it and could kick myself for staying away. Cape Cod, especially Orleans, is a very special place for me."

"Well, I can see why you would say that. This is breath-taking. All of it," he says, running his hand through his curly sandy-blond hair and grinning at Emma. "I wish I could spend more time here. But unfortunately, I need to get going. We're being fitted for our tuxes today and then organized events for the rest of the week. I wish people would do destination weddings. You fly in, watch them say I do, and you fly home. It was nice to run into you, Emma Callahan. I hope it's not the last time."

He pops his earbuds back in, turns, and jogs down the beach away from her. Emma's gaze follows him, her heart skipping a beat as he turns around, running backwards a few steps, smiles, and waves. Out of the corner of her eye she catches sight of her friends, their mouths hanging open in disbelief, leaning forward in their beach chairs, gesturing for her to hurry back to them.

"We aren't done with you Esme, but Emma, who was that gorgeous person you were talking to?"

"Just some guy. He was the best man at a wedding we did in April. He just stopped to say hi. Who wants to go for a swim?"

"Let's do it. I'm sick of talking about me," Esme says.

"Oh yeah? Since when? Race you," Emma says, getting a head start as Esme and Ellenor run after her, laughing.

The three best friends race to the water, dive into the waves, and scream in unison, "Summer Solstice!"

"The sunsets here never disappoint," Ellenor says later that evening as she stirs the ashes in their small bonfire. "This is so special—the three of us being together for another solstice, here on our beach, sitting around a fire, just like we used to do. I always loved the ritual of bonfires on this night."

"I forget, what's the connection between bonfires and the solstice?"

"Esme, how could you forget?" Ellenor says. "The bonfires help banish demons and evil spirits. The magic is the strongest tonight, so be gone, all you demons." She laughs, waving a stick in the air.

"Emma, take some pictures as a memento for all of us," Esme says. "Then, next year we will remember why the bonfires are important."

She pulls her camera out of her bag and starts snapping

pictures of the sunset and her friends. "Okay, let's crowd in. No—I want the ocean behind us. Good. Okay, everyone smile. Say 'Summer Solstice!'"

Chapter Fifteen

"There's nothing more beautiful than the way
the ocean refuses to stop kissing the
shoreline, no matter how many times
it's sent away." — Sarah Kay

Friday

"Good morning. Time to wake up. Summer rule number one—no sleeping in." As Esme shuffles her bare feet across the kitchen floor, she adds with a grumble, "Will I ever be able to sleep in?"

Emma opens one eye and then the other, pulling the quilt up close to her chin. She reflects on yesterday's events, grateful to have survived another Summer Solstice. As the designated beach driver, she maintained some sobriety. After swimming and lunch, she took a nap, dozing off to the sound of the waves, the gulls, and Esme and Ellenor's voices, soft and sweet. Her thoughts drift to Esme and the conversation they had regarding Cody and their marriage. *Would she actually leave him, or is this a midlife crisis? A very early midlife crisis?* Emma then remembers another part of the day and smiles. *That cute running guy—what's his name? Dammit, why can't I remember names?* He was the first person to make her heart beat a little faster since Ethan. *Screw Ethan.* She kicks off the quilt and gets out of bed.

The kitchen is cold. Cape Cod mornings, summer or not, can be deceiving. The sun is shining, but the air is cool. She pours herself a cup of coffee, thanks to Esme for brewing up a pot, then finds her out on the back deck.

"Good morning," she whispers. The breathtaking view demands a soft, quiet voice. This morning, the ocean is a stunning deep blue, almost indigo. The waves are sparkling like scattered diamonds under the bright sun. The dune grass sways gracefully in the gentle breeze, and the white sand forms a seamless carpet rolling out to meet the water's edge. Mother Nature has officially declared it—summer has arrived.

Esme looks up. "Good morning," she whispers back.

They sit side by side, silently sipping their coffees. Emma is lost in her own thoughts of growing up on Cape Cod and knows Esme must be as well. Their memories may differ, but they each hold in their hearts the feeling of warm sand beneath their feet, the first shock of diving into the ice-cold ocean. They were free spirits roaming the beaches, collecting shells and rocks, browned by the sun, always barefoot. They were the wild children running through the dunes, embracing the changes each season brought to them, excited by the sight of a seal, mesmerized by coyotes in the bogs, lulled to sleep by the sound of the waves. It would be years before the outside world would begin to sneak in, trying to wash away the joy of their childhood.

Ellenor stumbles out to the back deck, her eye mask, around her neck. She mumbles, "Good morning. Do either of you have asprin?" She sinks into a deck chair, spilling some of her coffee. "Shit, that's hot."

"Girl, if you ever get into a serious relationship, you are going to need some new sleeping attire. That's what you slept in the other night—and wore to the beach yesterday."

"If she does get into a serious relationship, she's not going to need sleeping attire," Emma says with a giggle, using air quotes for "sleeping attire."

"Maybe I am in a serious relationship," Ellenor murmurs, looking out at the ocean.

"What?" Emma and Esme shriek at the same time.

"Oh no, not again. Yesterday morning, Esme dropped a bombshell on us, and now you do it this morning? Tell us everything."

Ellenor responds, quietly, "I'm not ready to talk about it. It's very new, and I don't know where it might go, if anywhere. Please don't push me on this one. Please."

Esme speaks first. "Of course, Ell, of course." She nods her head, affirming her words.

"When and if you're ready to tell us, you know where to find us. Who wants more coffee?"

Esme pauses on her way into the house to bend forward and kiss Ellenor on the top of her head. It's a slight gesture, but it has such deep meaning to them, one they have shared since they were children. A kiss on the head lets them know they are loved and safe. A kiss on the head reassures them they aren't alone.

"Someone's texting you." Esme steps out onto the deck and hands Emma her cell phone.

"Gawd, it's eight in the morning. Who would dare to

text—oh, it's my pain-in-the-butt baby sister, Mo. My parents want to have breakfast with us. What do you guys think?"

"Of course. When? I think I need to jump in the ocean to clear my head," says Ellenor.

"In an hour. Oh, and they want us to do the cooking."

"You mean they want me to do the cooking, which I'm more than happy to do," Esme says. "Let me see what we've got for breakfast food. I'll come up with something fabulous."

Breakfast doesn't disappoint.

"Esme, I don't know how you can take a piece of bread and turn it into a delicacy," George Callahan says, sopping up the last piece of sourdough French toast with Vermont maple syrup. "It's damn good, and it's not even Sunday." He finishes his glass of freshly squeezed orange juice, leans back in his kitchen chair, and grins. "Having you three sitting around the table brings back such wonderful memories—I feel thirty years younger."

"I think you have on rose-colored glasses, dear. These girls were a handful. And I have the pictures to prove it," Betsey Callahan says before getting up from the table.

"You do? What pictures?" chirp the three of them. They spent the next forty-five minutes going through old pictures, laughing, reminiscing, and poking fun at each other.

"Look at this one. I think you were about six when you all insisted on being matching mermaids for Halloween. Ellenor, I don't know how your mother pulled off making those costumes, but she did a wonderful job. See? You all match, just like you demanded. And I do mean demanded. Honestly, all you three did was talk about being mermaid sisters and how you looked like each other. Truth be told, you looked nothing alike."

Betsey is silent for a minute, staring at the Halloween photo in her hand. She looks up at Esme, Ellenor, and Emma and smiles. Despite being in her late seventies, Betsey Callahan is a striking woman, her face etched with a lifetime of experiences, revealing a natural beauty and a testament to a life well-lived.

"Esme, look how cute you were. You're still cute. Your curls drove your mother berserk. She wanted them to behave the same way she wanted you to behave. But what I would have given to have hair like yours," she says, running her hand through her short gray hair. "I remember how the summer sun would lighten your caramel hair to a beautiful golden shade in no time. Oh, and your pouty lips and heart-shaped face made you look like an angel, but you didn't fool me. I could see storm clouds in those big brown eyes of yours when you didn't have your way. You certainly had a mind of your own.

"Emma, I don't know which of you girls were more determined to convince the world you were mermaid sisters, but you were a pain in the neck to live with then. You would stick out that determined little chin of yours and say, 'Mermaids don't eat that.' 'Mermaids don't sleep on a bed.' Mermaids don't do this, and mermaids don't do that. Good Lord, you went on and on."

She took a moment, seeming to fall into the memories of Emma's younger self. Tapping her finger on the old photograph, she continued, "You have the same personality and characteristics as Grandma Callahan. When she was younger, she had your hair—jet black and straight as a pin. Out of all my girls, your eyes are the spitting image of hers. I remember one day, sitting on the beach with a group of other mothers when you were about twelve months old. They were trying to pin a color to your eyes. Violet blue is the best description, I think. You were all arms and legs for so long I wondered if you would ever grow into your limbs, but you did." She smiled. "Emma, my beautiful, strong girl, never forget your inner strength, my dear."

She stares intently at the picture again. "Ellenor, you were the spitting image of your brother Delle. Even at three, we knew you were going to be tall. You both have such beautiful blond hair, and your eyes would change with the color of the ocean, from blue to gray. Your facial features are almost identical—strong profile with a perfect Roman nose, same high cheekbones, those gorgeous, thick brown brows."

"I used to hate them."

"I know you did, dear, but Brook Shields had nothing on you, and she was a model. I marveled at how you didn't burn with your milky white skin. Although I think you added an extra freckle to your nose every summer." She says this with a soft, warm smile, reaching out to touch Ellenor's hand.

"Have you been to see your father yet?"

"No, not yet. I suppose today is as good as any day. Have you seen him around town?"

"We run into Delle and Red from time to time, and we

always see Ordelle at every town meeting," interjects Mr. Callahan.

"Is he still a troublemaker?"

"Ordelle Snow is one of a kind, salt of the earth. He's done well sticking to his roots, raising a family, and not bowing down to anyone, let alone our town selectman. I sure enjoy it when he gets up to speak at the town meetings," he says with a snicker.

"Yup, that sounds like Dad," Ellenor says, clearly dreading the visit. "What did I expect? He'll never change."

"Emma, Esme, what are your plans for today? I don't want to play the mother card, but from the color on the three of you, you might want to avoid the sun today."

"I don't have any plans, Mom. Is there something you want to do?"

"I have a doctor's appointment in Hyannis—Maureen is taking us—and then I thought we could go to Whole Foods to stock up before the tourists descend, if they haven't already done so."

Maureen looks from her sister to her mother, prompting Emma to ask, "Mo, do you want me to come along?"

"Thanks, but you're here for such a quick visit, and Mom's doctor's appointment shouldn't be on your vacation agenda. No offense, Mom," she says, clearing the dishes from the table.

"None taken, dear. Your help is always appreciated." She says this with a quick glance at Emma, who looks from her sister to her father.

Was that a dig?

Breaking the underlying tension in the kitchen, Betsey

Callahan asks, "Esme, what are your plans for the day? How is your mother doing? I haven't seen her in years."

Esme ignores the question about her mother. "I need to do a quick run-through at CBI for the wedding tomorrow. Emma, why don't you come with me? I won't be too long, and afterward we can walk around downtown Chatham and do some retail therapy. Ellenor, how about you text us after you visit with your father? We can meet in Chatham, or better yet, maybe we can head to the Wellfleet Beachcomber. You won't believe who's playing there later today."

"The Casuals?

"Yup, the band is doing a reunion tour. God help us."

Chapter Sixteen

"I had a very dysfunctional family, and a very
hard childhood. So I made a world out of
words. And it was my salvation."
— Mary Oliver

Ellenor

Ellenor bears left out of the Callahan's driveway and
heads to Pochet Peninsula, her childhood home. She
drives past the Old Pequod Inn and grins. *A lot of memories
in that old place.*

The building was originally a grand sea captain's
mansion, built in 1857 and loved by generations of the
same family until it was sold in 1940. For a while, it served
as an inn, eventually housing the influx of college students
employed for summer on the Cape. After a change of
ownership and renovations, the Old Pequod Inn has been a
long-standing restaurant in Orleans.

She laughs to herself, remembering when she and
Emma waited tables there. They were both convinced the
place was haunted when they hid on the empty third floor
to smoke pot between customers.

As she approaches Pochet Bridge, Ellenor opens the

sunroof, anticipating the smell of salt air, and she isn't disappointed. The smell combines nostalgia, hope, and heartache. She takes a right onto the long dirt road to her father's house. So much has changed since the last time she was here. Quaint summer cottages have been torn down and replaced with trophy homes, and the ones left look like sitting ducks, waiting for the bulldozers to send them into oblivion. *At least the road isn't paved yet. These houses are like the bullies in high school, all in your face, look at me, look at poor you. And why on earth do you need an in-ground pool when you can walk to the ocean? What the fuck is wrong with people?* Ellenor's head is throbbing.

She slows the car, coming to the end of the road and the house she grew up in. Ellenor turns into the driveway and parks in front of a large scallop boat up on blocks. The red bottom paint is peeling, and the distinction between the blue and white paint on the hull has faded over the years. The gray shingled house, weathered and faded, looks as worn and tired as the boat parked next to it. To the left, rectangular wire lobster traps, stacked six feet high and wide, obscure the three bleached-out dories lying upside down, resembling beached dolphins. She looks around for her mother's vegetable garden, but all that remains is a wild, unruly patch of weeds, honeysuckle, milkweed, and ivy. Only a few weathered, broken pieces of the once-white picket fence remain, lying scattered on the ground around the old garden. *Mom would be heartbroken if she saw this. I think her garden and the beach were the only places she was truly at peace. She had her hands full with us as kids. I wonder how she had any energy or time for anything other than working at the restaurant and dealing with us. 'Wild indians,' she would call us. But one positive thing I remember is her telling us each to 'go for the gold' and to 'always treasure the Cape.' Well, Mama, I am getting very close to the gold—not sure about the other part.* As she turns off the ignition, a figure appears from under the scallop boat.

"Isn't that thing supposed to be in the water by now?" she says, stepping out of the car.

"Supposed to be, but it isn't. Aren't you supposed to be in San Francisco, little sister?"

"Supposed to be, but I'm not," Ellenor says, walking toward her brother. "How are you, Red?"

Her older brother walks over to her, smiling. "I'm doing good right now. You are a sight for sore eyes. I didn't know you were coming."

"I thought I'd surprise Dad. Speaking of surprises, what's that?" she says, shading her eyes and pointing to a house in mid-construction across from her father's.

"New house."

"Dad's building a new house?" Ellenor frowns at her brother, and she is pretty sure Red sees the confusion written on her face.

Red sighs and runs his hand through his strawberry blond hair sprinkled with red paint flakes. "No, Ell. Dad sold a few acres. We have neighbors now, or we will once that trophy house is finished."

"What do you mean? Dad sold a few acres?" Ellenor feels nauseous, and not from the lingering hangover. "I don't understand. He would never do that."

Red wipes his hands on his dusty jeans. "Well, he did, and it's done. Nothing can change that now."

Ellenor shakes her head back and forth. "No, that can't be right. Why? Why didn't anyone tell me? Why the hell would he do that? Dad said he would never sell."

"He needed the money. It's as simple as that. The real estate taxes have gone sky high with a slew of these damn monster homes being built. And now we have to deal with flood insurance—as insane as that sounds. That ocean isn't going to swallow up our house in our lifetime, but apparently, the State-of-Massachusetts insurance assholes assume it will."

"Why didn't you tell me? Why didn't Dad tell me? I might've been able to help. This is horrible, on so many levels. What the hell, Red? Why didn't someone stop him?" she says, her voice rising as she surveys the property in disbelief.

Red kicks at a faded oyster shell in the dirt driveway before saying, "Have you been gone for so long that you've forgotten what Dad is like? Let me remind you—he's bull-headed, proud, stubborn, and arrogant. The only way is his way. I'm not sure how much longer he can hold on to the other twelve acres. Do you know how much this property can sell for? He could retire and never worry about money for the rest of his life. Truth be told, we would all benefit if he sold the whole place."

Ellenor rubs the back of her right shoulder, the tension building up in her tight muscles. "Is he home?"

She walks to the front door, which had once been painted a beautiful shade of robin egg blue, her mother's favorite color. When her father complained, "That's a color for girls." She answered, "Everyone likes blue—it feels soft, like the pillows on your bed after a long hard day of work." He smiled and said, "Can you paint the back door the same color?" Now the door is weathered and cracked like the scales on an alligator's back, faded, the color barely there.

Ellenor hesitates, questioning her decision to come back to this house. *Do I knock or just walk in?* She slowly opens the screen door. "Dad, are you home?"

The living room hasn't changed since she lived here, only now the space is worn, tired, and just plain-old dirty looking. Two dogs jump off the plaid sofa and slowly walk over to meet her. Ellenor is glad to see them—older but still around.

She couches down to pat them. "Hi guys. I've missed you." *This is why it's so dirty in here. Two black labs bringing in sand and dirt and shedding like crazy. Does anyone vacuum, or at the very least, sweep up?*

"Who's here?"

Ellenor braces herself, not sure what to expect. *Has he aged? Have I aged?*

Will he kick me out? Will he even recognize me? Five years is a long time. People change.

Ordelle Snow walks into the living room and stops in his tracks when he sees Ellenor bent down patting the dogs. "Ellenor?"

She looks up at her father. He is still tall, standing erect, tanned as always, but his face has weathered—the lines are deeper. His hair is still the same, other than a few more grays scattered across his trademark crew cut. All her life,

Ellenor overheard conversations about someone complaining about a local fisherman, and the response would be, "If he has a crew cut, that would be Ordelle Snow."

"Hi, Dad. Yup, it's me, Ellenor," she says. They stand there awkwardly, assessing each other, with the dogs between them.

"This is a surprise. Why didn't you call? I would have cleaned up. Are you hungry? We might have something I can pull together."

"I'm not hungry, Dad, but thanks. Yeah, sorry I didn't call, but my schedule is so unpredictable I wasn't sure when I could get here. How are you? You haven't changed a bit."

"The last time I saw you was at your mother's funeral. I know damn right well I've changed. We've all changed, your brothers and me. Nothing is the same since she's been gone. But you, you look pretty much the same as you did then. Still have that short hair of yours. God, your mother was heartbroken when you cut off your hair. Tell me again why you did that?"

"It doesn't matter anymore. And hey, it's easy, just like your hair."

They both smile.

"Are you thirsty? There's some iced tea in the fridge if you're planning on visiting for a while."

Ellenor, the dogs, and Ordelle sit out on the back deck, which is as worn and faded as everything around them, except for the breathtaking view. The deck overlooks Pochet Inlet and the dunes out to the Atlantic Ocean. The Callahans' view is spectacular, but this landscape is the wild part of the beach—the part tourists can't access unless they want to walk miles in the burning sand to see what Ellenor grew up with. Ten miles of pristine shoreline, a land untouched by development and revered by the locals.

Ellenor shifts in the Adirondack chair. In a controlled voice, she says, "Why didn't you tell me you were thinking about selling some of the land?"

"Why should I? You weren't around, and didn't seem like you were ever coming around again, so what business is it of yours?" Ordelle responds in a matter-of-fact tone.

"I might have been able to help if I had known. We could have all put our heads together and come up with a plan." She wishes she could just get up and leave, but Ellenor is certain that if she does, she will never be welcomed back.

"How could you have helped? You don't even work, from what I can tell."

"I do work, Dad, you know that. I'm an author. I get paid to write, and I get paid a lot of money. If only you had called me before you started breaking this place up. My God, do you realize what you have here? You have a fucking piece of paradise, and you are willing to just sell it off?" Ellenor realizes she's raising her voice but can't seem to control herself.

Ordelle's face is red. He points a finger at her, saying, "Watch your language. Yeah, I know all about your writing, and that's not a proper job—you aren't earning a real living. It's a goddamn hobby. And I know exactly what I have here. If you were around more often, you would too. Bills, bills, and more bills."

Ellenor remains silent, trying to process the situation, the words. The memories are all flooding into her brain, threatening to drown her.

"Look, it doesn't matter what you think about how I make my money, but I make money, I earn real money, I earn a real living." She feels herself ready to step over the line, but something pulls her back in. "I could have helped you financially. This is—or was—my home too. But it's still your home, and you're still my father, so let me help. How can I help? Pay the real estate bills, or maybe the insurance? Let me help." She feels like a kid pleading for permission to stay out late.

Ordelle stands up and walks to the deck railing, looking out over his land to the ocean he loves. He grew up here. This was his father's property, and back then, what was eighteen acres, most of it oceanfront, was whittled down to the fifteen he left for Ordelle. Now he's down to twelve acres, and soon it will be less.

"Ellenor," he says, still looking out to the ocean, "I appreciate the sentiment, but I don't need your help. Your brothers and I are doing just fine."

"From where I'm sitting, it doesn't look that way to me. You've got a worn-down scallop boat sitting in the driveway instead of being tied up to a slip in the harbor, ready to work. Red told me a while back you sold the charter boat, so that's a hit to your income. How long will the money last from selling off those acres? Something's got to give, Dad. I can help."

"I told you I don't want your goddamn help!" he roars, slamming his hand on the deck railing. With a brittle laugh, he says, "It was nice of you to stop by, but I need to get some things done around here. Write when you find proper work."

Ellenor bit her lip to keep her tears at bay. "Okay. See ya, Dad." She doesn't know if he turns to watch her walk away—she doesn't look back at him. Thoughts of her carefree days growing up on the beach with her brothers and parents linger as she gets into her car. Her mind flashes to herself as a little girl trying to keep up with her brothers, pail in hand, while they combed the beach for lost lures and buoys that had washed up on the shore. Ordelle Snow could take someone else's lost or tossed-out items and put them to good use. In those times, little Ellenor would give anything to find a shiny lure that her brothers had missed, hoping her treasure would make her dad proud of her.

She puts the car in reverse and drives away from what was her home to the place she's most at home, the Callahan's.

Chapter Seventeen

"Planning is the art of pretending you have control over the universe." – Alan W. Watts

Chatham Beach Inn

"Did you notice anything different about Mo this morning?" Emma asks, opening the passenger door of the Audi.

"Other than your little sister's usual woe-is-me Eeyore face?"

"I don't know, I can't put my finger on it, but something is up with her."

Esme shrugs as she checks herself out in the rearview mirror and adjusts her sunglasses. She puts the Audi in drive, selects Bruno Mars from her playlist and heads down the shore road to the Chatham Beach Inn. They pull into the wide circular drive surrounded by a hedge of over-flowing hydrangeas. The large round flower heads, a blue as vibrant as the ocean, seem to float over the canopy of dense green foliage.

"This place has always intimidated me. It's such an

understated level of ultra-rich. What the hell does it cost to have a wedding here?"

"Don't let it intimidate you. We look the part in this car, and I know exactly what it costs to have a wedding here. I have the invoice ready to hand to the bride's daddy."

Esme steps out from the flashy red convertible in her Jimmy Choo platform wedges and hands the keys to the waiting valet. The shoes add just enough height, accentuating her already long legs emerging gracefully from her floral-print Lily Pulitzer sheath dress. Esme is confident and drop-dead gorgeous, and she owns it. Emma, on the other hand, wishes she had stayed home. *I could be helping my mother with the breakfast dishes, maybe dusting the pollen off the furniture—anything but this.*

"Are you coming?"

"Yes, and by the way, you sound like your mother," Emma hisses as she comes around to the driver's side of the car.

"Good. Let's go."

Two can play this game. Emma releases her shiny jet-black hair from her scrunchie and gives it a shake, knowing it will land directly below her shoulders. She smiles, looking at Esme's mess of curls. Adorable as they may be, it's Emma's hair that commands attention, highlighting her striking violet eyes and perfectly symmetrical face. Her pink Tory Burch polo shirt and classic white pleated tennis skirt create a look of effortless sophistication, perfectly complemented by her playful pink-flamingo Toms. *All I need is a diamond tennis bracelet, and I would fit right in.*

They walk side by side up the wide stairway, through

the double doors, and into the luxurious foyer of Chatham Beach Inn.

Esme stops to look at a text. "I have to meet the bride's parents at the beach bar. Come with me. You can mingle with the idle rich at the bar while I work. I need to do a quick overview with them, walk the perimeter, go over any last-minute changes, pray there aren't any, then I am done."

"Moët, please." *It's not every day that I get to see things from the other side, so why not take this time to enjoy it while I can?*

Emma gazes out at the water from the beach bar, lost in her memories. Across a small inlet lies a spit of sand, referred to as the Outer Beach by the locals. Sitting here, sipping her champagne, she pictures her parents strategically packing up their old Willys, long before they had the Jeep, for their weekend trips to a friend's cottage on the Outer Beach. Nobody grumbled about going, even though her older sisters usually despised family outings. But this was different, and they all knew it. They would drive up to the Heights and pick up Esme. She was always out front, alone, with her sleeping bag, pillow, and overnight bag. Then they would drive to Pochet to pick up Ellenor. An older brother was always waiting with her. While Esme looked defiant in her lack of parental supervision, Ellenor looked embarrassed to have someone standing next to her, as if she couldn't take care of herself. Mr. and Mrs. Callahan never commented on either child's circumstances—they simply gave each other a knowing smile and said, "Find room in the back."

"Hey there, Emma?"

She turns to the sound of her name. *Holy shit, it's that beach hunk.*

"Well, hi there. So we meet again."

"Yeah, maybe kismet, huh? I would ask if you're staying here, but considering where you live, this would be slumming for you."

She smiles. *What the hell is his name?* "You are right, I'm not staying here, and you are right again, I am slumming." She laughs, surprised at how she flirts so easily with this guy. *What's his name?*

"Do you mind if I join you?"

"Please do." She motions to the bartender. "Excuse me, when you have a chance, this gentleman would like a glass of Moët. My tab please."

He pulls out the bar stool next to her, looking casual in a pair of long classic-fit navy blue shorts and a white T-shirt. He seems incredibly comfortable in his skin, not caring what he's wearing or who may be looking at him.

"Thanks, but you don't need to pay for it. Unless, of course, you have a room tab going." He is funny, flirtatious, and very sexy.

Emma swings around on her bar stool to face him, fully aware that her knees—her naked knees—are almost touching his naked knees. "So, what are you doing here?"

"I was about to ask you the same question. I'm here for a wedding. The bride knows us all too well. We were summoned to arrive days early to make sure we were all accounted for, on time, and presentable for the ceremony."

"How's that plan working?"

"Only time will tell. We still have twenty-four hours to

screw up before they say 'I do.'" He raises his glass of Moët in her direction, flashing his dazzling smile, then says in a mischievous tone, "That's my story, so what's yours? What about you—why aren't you home patrolling that beach of yours?"

Ben! That's his name. "I hope I didn't give the wrong impression. It's not only *my* beach, although I like to think it is." She pauses for a second, appreciating how easy she feels sitting here with this handsome stranger.

"I'm here with a friend. She's checking on some last-minute details for a wedding she's catering tomorrow. How ironic if it's your wedding?"

Looking at her in mock horror, he says, "Let me be perfectly clear, it's not my wedding." They laugh, clinking their champagne glasses, then smile at each other.

"All jokes aside, it's wonderful to see you again. I kept thinking about you yesterday. Honestly, I haven't stopped thinking about you since my brother's wedding. I even checked you out on your website."

"Sounds a bit stalkerish to me," Emma says, finishing her glass. She is about to order another one when she hears her name. Esme is walking toward her, phone to her ear, obviously on a mission.

"Here you are. I've been texting you. Did you lose your phone or something?"

Emma looks around for a minute. "Damn, I hope it's in the car, with my purse."

She looks over at her hunky beach friend and says, sheepishly, "It appears the drinks are on you. I'm sorry."

Esme gapes from Emma to the man she's talking to. *Is that the guy from the beach yesterday? It can't be.* "Emma, we need to go. Ell needs us."

"Wait, you can't just leave me with the bar tab. That's called something. I don't know what, but I know it's something."

"Sorry, but I've got to go. I know this look, and she means business."

He jumps off the bar stool. "Come to the wedding tomorrow. Be my plus-one. Please, I can't imagine that the fates would have us meet twice in two days only to never see each other again."

God, that's romantic. Who is this guy? And wedding? What wedding?

"Did you just invite her to a wedding? What wedding?" Esme narrows her eyes, homing in on the handsome stranger.

"Here, tomorrow. Come on Emma, it will be fun. Well, sorta fun. Please."

"The wedding is here? Tomorrow? You wouldn't be talking about the Bauer wedding?"

"Yup, that's the one. I'm in the wedding."

Then in unison, he and Emma say, "Always the groomsman, never the groom," and start laughing.

Esme is standing in her perfect Jimmy Choo's, at a loss for words. *What the hell is happening here? Who is this person, and how can he and Emma already have a private joke?* "I'm terribly sorry, but Emma won't be joining you." She raises her hand like a crossing guard for kindergarteners. "No, no, not a comment that requires a response. You see, I am the caterer, and I know *exactly* how many dinners and drinks have been paid for, and there isn't a dime left for a plus one." She turns to Emma. "Come on, we need to go—now."

"Honestly, Esme, that was rude the way you spoke to Ben," Emma says as she fastens her seat belt, relieved to see her purse in the back seat.

"Sorry. I know I came across strong. I'm worried about Ell—her texts are cryptic. We both know how her family can send her spiraling. That was the guy from the beach yesterday, right?" Emma nods and puts her hair back into a ponytail. Her thoughts drift to Ben as Esme drives them home.

"We're out back!" Ellenor shouts from the Callahan's back deck.

"Here you are. Hi, Dad, how'd the doctor's appointment go?"

Mr. Callahan shifts in his chair.

"It went fine," Mo says before her father can answer.

"Where's Mom? Ell, why didn't you meet us in Chatham?"

"I had a typical visit with my dad, and your mother's upstairs resting. Have a seat and I'll fill you in."

Over freshly made lemonade, Ellenor updates her friends about how her father sold some of the property, which already has a house being built on it, and that he's considering selling the rest to pay the taxes and insurance.

"He's so darn stubborn, and he won't take help from

anyone. It would be devastating for him, and us, if he loses the land. We got into it, and as usual, he pretty much told me to leave. That's when I came here, to your parents'." She glances over at Mr. Callahan, smiling. Ever since she was a child, the Callahan's home has been a safe haven for her, away from the mayhem of her parents' home. "We were just putting our heads together to see what can be done to save that property from being developed."

"A conservation trust is a great option," Mo says. "That's what we did here."

Emma looks at her younger sister. "You did what?"

"Mom and Dad put the property into a conservation trust. This way, our land is protected. We can never build on it, but that's a small price to pay for peace of mind."

She looks from her father to her sister, bewildered. "What are you talking about? When did this happen? Why don't I know about it?" she says in a strained voice.

Emma's dad smiles with that all-knowing Mr. Callahan look. "We'd been thinking about it for years when the property taxes kept increasing, and then the insurance companies started to turn away people who didn't carry flood insurance. So we got an attorney and came up with a plan. We drew up a deed with the attorney to create an open space easement. The property is still ours and always will be, but we agreed to not add any more cottages. This way, we got a nice chunk of change, and the land is protected as open space."

"An easement? So can people simply come walk across our yard? Why didn't you guys tell me about this?" Despite her attempt at appearing calm, Emma's voice gives her away.

"It's not a big deal. Nobody can walk across our yard, and we didn't tell you because you were going through a rough time yourself." Mo appears uncomfortable, as if bringing up Emma's divorce might send her back down a black hole.

Esme glances at her watch. *This may be a good time to get out of here.* "Hey, if we are going to do that thing, we should think about changing and leaving soon."

"You're right. Thanks for talking about all of this with me, Mr. Callahan. I feel better about things. Of course, it remains to be seen how my father and brothers will react to the idea of putting the property into a trust."

Emma kisses her dad on the cheek and gives Mo a cryptic look, then the three walk back to their cottage in silence.

Chapter Eighteen

"Some things are so unexpected that no one is
prepared for them." – Leo Rosten

Musings

E sme is up early again, and again, it's for work. "This is getting old, and so am I," she says to no one, arriving at CBI at eight in the morning. She's pleased to see the large tent is set up on the south lawn, taking advantage of the panoramic views of the ocean. Under the tent, the dance floor is surrounded by round tables draped in cream French-linen tablecloths. Every table is meticulously set with gold-rimmed dinner plates, gold cutlery, crisp pink linen napkins, and crystal glassware. Crystal vases filled with white tea roses and blush peonies and gold taper candle holders with thin pink candles add to the overall theme of classic elegance.

"This looks just as I imagined," Esme says out loud as she notices Roseanne walking toward her. She sees the rest of her team in catering mode, busy setting up the mimosa bar for the guests.

"Good morning, boss," Roseanne says. She leans in for a hug and whispers, "I hate everyone." She gives Esme a fake smile.

"You look adorable in pink. It goes so well with your purple hair."

"My hair is not purple—it's magenta." Roseanne hisses.

Esme laughs. "I'm getting used to that wild color. I have to admit, it complements your beautiful olive skin and dark eyes. To each to their own, Roseanne, to each their own."

The bride and her mother insisted that all staff, regardless of who they are, must wear pink polo shirts tucked into crisp khakis. Esme never said yes or no to that stipulation. She sneers, looking up to the gray sky, silently wishing it would rain on this bride. She walks around the grounds in her pink linen sheath and white leather Dolce sneakers. This is her rebellious response to the uniforms—the sneakers are a practical choice to maneuver from a manicured lawn to a sandy beach and a slippery industrial kitchen floor, in case anyone asks.

From the sidelines, Esme watches the bride and her father walk down the aisle of freshly ground white seashells lined with eucalyptus leaves interlaced with delicate pink roses and baby's breath. "Those flowers must be dyed to match so perfectly," she says under her breath. The bridesmaids are wearing matching pink-floral Stella McCartney tea dresses, blush leather crisscross Prada ballet flats, and pearl necklaces and studs. *What the hell did their outfits cost? Stella McCartney? Prada? Really?*

The groomsmen are standing at attention in white linen

pants, pink-and-white-striped Oxford shirts, pink Vineyard Vines ties adorned with blue anchors, navy blue suit jackets, and sockless navy-blue topsiders. They look miserable.

Her mind wanders back to yesterday, which started out well but deteriorated to the day that may never be spoken of again. The slow descent began with Ellenor texting her an SOS. Then she found Emma flirting with the cute guy from the beach, who coincidently is a groomsman at this wedding. The conversation with Mr. C. about selling land, the insane property taxes, and the high cost of living on the Cape took the wind out of all of their sails. The original plan for the afternoon was to spend it at the Wellfleet Beach Comber, drinking and dancing to their favorite band, The Casuals, just like they did when they were younger. But they agreed they weren't in the mood for drunk dancing like twenty-year-olds at the Comber. Emma flat-out said, "I feel too old to pretend we fit in." They admitted that sometimes they felt old and that this was one of those times. Instead of drinking and dancing the afternoon away, they opted for an afternoon swim and an early dinner on the lawn of the Old Pequod Inn. They biked to the inn, settled themselves into the Adirondack chairs that were scattered about the lawn, and ordered a bottle of Veuve Clicquot.

"If we are going to be sensible and act like adults, we might as well be rich adults who know how to drink fine champagne." Esme smiled.

They'd agreed not to talk about anything that would sour their moods—in other words, just about anything that related to the recent events of the day. Two bottles of

Veuveand a few dozen Wellfleet oysters later, they were lost in laughter, Emma and Ellenor sharing stories of their summers waitressing at the Inn.

"Oh my God, we would get stoned before our shift and wonder why our tips sucked." Ellenor almost spilled her glass telling the story.

Esme sighs. *Everything was going so well.* That is, until Ethan showed up with two of Ellenor's brothers. She spotted them first and hoped they would go inside to the bar or, better yet, leave unnoticed. *I should have just grabbed Emma and ran before stupid Delle spotted us.*

"Hey, Ell, I heard you were in town," Delle said as he leaned over to kiss his sister on the cheek. "I also heard you got Dad all riled up. Hi, Esme, Emma."

Ellenor glared at Red, who had obviously filled their brother in on the morning's events.

"Yeah, about that, I might have a solution to help Dad save face while solving the land issue." Ellenor stood up, motioning for Delle and Red to move with her away from the group.

Esme remembers how uncomfortable she felt with Ethan standing there, looking like a complete idiot, unable to take his eyes off Emma. She wanted to jump up and slap him. They have known each other since they were kids. Esme thought of him as a brother. But last night she didn't recognize him. Not that he had aged more than expected—it was something else. *Was it the remaining stench of his cheating lies? His deceit? Was it how he had fooled us all?*

"Hi ladies, Emma. How are you?" he sputtered, pushing his hair out of his eyes.

Esme shakes her head. *What was Emma feeling then? I mean, she hadn't seen Ethan in five years, and then all of a sudden, he was standing in front of her.*

"I'm good," she mumbled, not looking up. "Esme, more champagne?"

Esme turned from Ethan to Emma, who was holding the bottle of Veuve Clicquot toward her. *I need to end this now.*

"No thanks. I think that bottle is about done, and so am I."

Esme cautiously watched Emma pour what was left in the bottle into her own glass.

She swallowed it in one gulp, and said defiantly, "This bottle might be done, but I'm only getting started."

The air was thick with emotion, as if a cold, damp fog had rolled in from the ocean and settled directly over the group of old friends.

Ethan shifted from one foot to the other, pushed his hair out of his eyes again, as if unsure of what to do, then in a strained voice said, "Hey, Esme, it's been a long time. How's Cody? How's CJ?"

He rubbed the back of his neck, shaking his head ever so slightly, and looked at Emma. "It's nice to see you, Emma—you look good. You haven't changed a bit. I didn't know you'd be here. We just came for a beer…" He stood there, looking hopeless. She didn't respond.

Ethan's voice was low, almost a whisper, as he said, "I think I'll go in and find a seat at the bar." He slowly turned and walked away.

Esme watches as the bride and groom kiss in front of

their cheering guests. She shakes her head to forget last night, but memories of the events that took place aren't going anywhere. After Ethan went into the Pequod Bar, Emma said she needed to pee and staggered a bit when she stood up. She tried to cover it up by straightening her shoulders and standing up straight. She may have fooled most, but Esme wasn't fooled one little bit.

"Me too. I'll come with you."

"Esme, I think I can go to the bathroom without a chaperone. I'll be right back. Anyway, you need to stay here so Ellenor doesn't think we've abandoned her." Esme watched Emma disappear inside the bar and looked around frantically for Ellenor.

There she is. Damn it, why is she still talking to Delle? He's the last person I want to see right now. Esme smiled when she realized she could text Ellenor and not have to engage with Delle. She was quite pleased with herself—SOS is all she texted. She watched Ellenor look down at her phone, look around to catch Esme's eye, say something to Delle, and head straight for her friend.

"Hey, what's up? Where's Emma?"

"Going to the 'bathroom.'" She made air quotes.

"So, that required an SOS?"

"Ethan is in the bar. If you remember, you have to walk through the bar to get to the bathrooms."

"Oh no."

"Yup. Let's go."

"Home? Without Emma?"

"For God's sake. No. We need to sneak into the bar

without being noticed and watch to see what happens. Hopefully, it's still as dark as it used to be. Come on."

Esme smirks to herself, remembering how they went in through the back door, a trick only the locals know about.

The bar was as dimly lit as Esme remembered, almost certainly to keep people drinking, not knowing if it was day or night. She and Ellenor pressed themselves against the wall, careful not to bump into any of the countless framed photographs that lined it. All the walls in the bar, painted in an off-white, are crowded with these photos—pictures of summer staff from years past, black-and-white photos of the regulars who are probably long gone, and lots of photos of the changes the Pequod Inn has gone through in the last one hundred years.

"There's Ethan, over by the fireplace," Esme whispered, pointing toward the massive stone fireplace the bar is known for. At that moment, Emma came out of the ladies' room and bumped into Ethan. Esme and Ellenor watched as the two exchanged words.

"What are they saying?"

"How should I know? I can't read lips," Esme hissed. She put her hand over Ellenor's mouth to stop her from talking.

"What on earth are you two doing? You both look as guilty as you did when you were teenagers up to no good."

"Shut up, Delle," Esme and Ellenor responded sharply.

This caused Ethan to turn abruptly, and he spotted the three of them lurking in the shadows in the bar's corner. He looked back at Emma, who had a silly, somewhat drunken grin on her face.

"Ah, my people are here," she said, arms outstretched, walking toward them.

Esme tried to get Emma to leave. "Come on, Em, let's get going. Remember, we have to ride bikes back to the house."

Emma shook Esme's hand off her arm. "I'm not going anywhere until I hear what Ethan has to say. You do have something to say to me, right, Ethan?" She swayed a bit, but that didn't stop her. "After all this time, I am sure you have something to say."

Ethan, clearly uncomfortable, softly said, "Sure, whatever you want. Let's have a seat, and I'll tell you everything." He looked at Delle, Ellenor, and Esme, who were staring at him. "Alone."

"Emma, come on," Esme said, reaching for her.

Emma spun around, clenched her fists, and stuck out her pointy chin. "No. I said I want to hear what he has to say, and I want you to hear it, too, because I probably won't remember a word of it tomorrow. Look, there's a table where we can all fit." She started walking toward the table.

The others stood there, unsure of what to do.

Ellenor motioned to a server. "Is it okay if we sit over there? Either way, we want a bottle of Patrón and five shot glasses."

"Sure, do you want salt and lime with that?"

"Nope, but knock yourself out and bring us a round of water." She tilted her head to her side, and with a sheepish grin, she apologized, knowing her comment was uncalled for. "I'm sorry. I didn't mean to come off as a bitch. It's obvious that we have a situation here. I didn't mean to take it out on you."

The server looked confused.

Ellenor motioned toward Esme. "That one has a temper, though. She likes to break things."

"Oh, for God's sake, don't listen to her. Please bring a pitcher of water. I'm working tomorrow, if anyone cares, and somebody needs to be the grownup here. So, let's sit down, everyone, and listen to what Ethan has to say."

The five of them hesitated around the old oblong wooden table, unsure where to sit, but as always, Esme took charge with a self-satisfied huff. "Emma, you sit next to me. Ellenor, you're next to Emma. Ethan and Delle, you can sit on the other side."

Ethan remained standing. "There is no way that I can do this. This is a conversation between Emma and me, nobody else. You agree with me, right Emma?"

Esme frowns. She is sure she saw Emma focus in on Delle before responding to Ethan. *Did he give Emma a discreet little nod, or did I imagine that?* Esme shakes her head, attempting to return to the present moment and concentrate on the wedding, but the images from last night refuse to fade. She can't stop thinking about Delle, who looked so damn handsome last night. He was aging well— still had that rugged look and those damn unpredictable blue-gray eyes, just like Ellenor's.

Emma pulled out her chair, sat down, and said, "You have the floor, Ethan. We all want to hear what you have to say." Just then, the server delivered the bottle of Patrón, five shot glasses, a pitcher of water, and five glasses with ice.

"Thank you," Ellenor said, smiling at the nervous server, and motioned for Delle to start pouring.

Ethan's elbows were on the table, his chin resting in his hands. He scanned the table, his blue eyes pleading for someone to stop this. He reached for the glass, downed the shot of Patrón, wiped his mouth with the back of his hand, then began.

"This is… this is really hard to talk about. I'm embarrassed and ashamed of what I've done."

"Keep going," Ellenor said, refilling everyone's shot glasses.

"Okay, but no interruptions, please. I just need to get through this." He shifted his gaze to Emma, who was scowling and biting her lip. "Sorry, what I meant is I need to make things clear. Emma, I love you. Nothing has changed that. I have always loved you—since we were kids. You were such a pain in the ass, and then you grew up and became my pain in the ass." Ethan gave a feeble half-smile and took another shot.

Just as he was about to begin again, Red walked up to the table. "Well, hey, y'all. This is where you wound up. I was looking for you." Red looked around for an empty chair to pull up to the table when Delle said, "Not now, Red— not a good time."

"What's that supposed to mean? We came here together, and now isn't a good time? Good time for what?" Red took off his well-worn Red Sox ball cap and ran his fingers through his shaggy strawberry-blond hair.

Esme stood up, filled a shot glass, and handed it to him.

"Here you go, Red. Swig it. There's a seat at the bar. Why don't you grab it, have a few more shots, and tell the bartender to put it on my tab? This is stuff you don't want to know about. Trust me." She gave Red a knowing look and patted him on his arm. "We'll catch up soon—promise."

Placated with the promise of good tequila, Red quickly downed the shot, adjusted his cap, and sulked over to the bar.

Emma spoke first. "How could you just get up and leave? Why did you leave? What happened? How could I not have known what was going on with you?" She gulped her shot, motioned for another one, and in a firm voice said, "We are all ears, Ethan."

Ethan ran his hand through his hair, straight and as black as Emma's. "I was unhappy. I felt like all I did was work, and then I'd come home to the same old thing." He realized immediately by the look on Emma's face that those were the wrong words. "I was going through something, maybe a midlife crisis. I was scared, I was getting older, and I thought there had to be more to life. I don't know. I knew Kaisa, we both did. She was nice, but she seemed to always be in the background. I didn't really talk to her beyond the usual 'hi, how ya doing?' kind of thing."

"That's because she was the fucking nanny, not the star of the day, Ethan."

Ethan closed his eyes and exhaled loudly. "I know Ellenor, believe me, I know. Anyway, to continue. At first, it was simply an innocent flirtation. I never meant for it to go any further. But then things started to heat up. Kaisa would come into the city on her days off and we'd have lunch or just walk around Central Park. She stroked my ego. She made me feel important, virile." He shook his head, embarrassed. "We both knew we wanted to be together, and we both knew what a bombshell it would be. I promised myself that I wouldn't cheat on you." He was struggling to look at Emma. Perhaps looking down seemed safer.

"Oh, how noble of you, Ethan. That makes everything so much better." Ellenor's words came out of her mouth like a ball of fire.

Ethan could barely look anyone in the face. "Ellenor, please let me get through this. I didn't have sex with her until after I left. She didn't want to wait, but she agreed to it and that made me feel masculine. I was in control. After I made the decision to leave and she quit her job, we got a studio apartment in the city. Things were good—I felt free. I felt like I used to. A weight was lifted off my shoulders. She never asked for things, like did I pay the mortgage? Did I think we should trade in the Volvo for a Land Rover? Did I know if we needed milk? She never asked for anything—she only wanted to please me, both emotionally and sexually."

Emma leaned over to Esme and whispered, "If I vomit on him, will I hit his shoes or his shirt?"

"Emmie, don't look at me like that. I can't bear to see the pain on your face. I was wrong, I was so fucking wrong, and I've been paying for this mistake, this huge mistake, for years." Emma slammed her hand on the table. "Don't you dare call me Emmie, and the look on my face is not pain.

It's a look of sheer and utter confusion. So, are you telling me you left me after how many years of marriage and a lifetime of friendship because I asked you if you paid the mortgage, or if we needed some fucking milk?"

Esme knew Emma was on the verge of losing control, but then her friend did something that surprised her—she took a deep breath and, in a tone dripping with scorn, said, "Where is your little Swedish slut—sorry—nanny? Are you afraid of bringing her out in public where people know you and know what you've done? Or is the age difference and the betrayal of one of their own something you would rather keep to yourself?"

Ethan turned his head, avoiding eye contact with everyone. He looked at the tequila and fingered his shot glass, but when Delle went to pour him another shot, he shook his head no. Ethan quietly murmured in a low voice, "Kaisa is gone. She's back in Sweden. She's been deported. The only reason she wanted to be with me was for me to marry her so she could get a green card. I got played. I'm a middle-aged dude who got all hot and bothered thinking this young blond thing was into me, for who I was. I was convinced that she was attracted to me, not what I could do for her. I am a goddamn loser idiot who lost the love of my life, and that's you, Emma."

Ellenor let out a snort, glaring at Ethan.

He reached for Emma's hand, and she let him take it before saying, "Ya know, I think that's bullshit, Ethan." She shrugged her shoulders, leaned in closer to him from across the table, and continued. "Who really has the love of their life? Like, how do you know who that is? Is it after you marry that person, pledging to love each other, or is it after they walk out on you?"

She pulled her hand away from his and raised it to stop him from saying anything. "When you left me, with no explanation, I was brought to my knees. For a while, I thought you were gay. Ya know, that would have been easier to understand than why you ran away with the neighbors' nanny. That's so cliché, but I didn't know that then, or maybe I didn't want to know it then. I couldn't understand what had happened. What had I done to make you leave?

"I was consumed by a fog of confusion—the devastation you left in your wake was like a physical blow to my body, my brain, my heart. The dark hopelessness I fought every day threatened to drown me. It took me a long time, and a lot of therapy, to understand that the question isn't 'Why did you leave me?' The question is and always will be 'What can I learn from this pain?' I needed to dig deep to figure it out, and I think I'm close. For a long time, I thought the pain of losing you, losing us, would crush me. But it didn't. You see, I replaced an I with an E."

Ethan looked at her then at the rest of them sitting silently, eyes glued on him. "Huh, an I with an E. What does that even mean?"

"I'm not *bitter* Ethan, I'm *better*, an I for an E, a simple change of a vowel." She stood up and looked at Esme and Ellenor. "Let's go." And with that, Emma Callahan bent down, let her long black hair fall around Ethan's face, and kissed him passionately on the lips. She stood back up, smiled a wicked smile, and said, "Goodbye, Ethan."

The three lifelong friends walked out the front door of

the Old Pequod Inn to Stevie Nicks' "Silver Springs" blaring on the music track.

"Esme, I think we should start to pass the apps, okay?"

She snaps back to the present and surveys the scene, and it is spectacular. The sky is still gray, but the view is breathtaking. The entire venue overlooks a white sandy beach and the calm blue waters of Aunt Lydia's Cove, which is protected from the Atlantic Ocean by the Cape Cod National Seashore's North Beach Island.

"Now is a perfect time to pass the apps. Thank you for checking in." She wanders on the perimeter of the festivities, watching for anything that may cause an issue for this bride and groom. While she may not have a genuine interest in either of them, she recognizes she has an obligation to be professional and ensure things flow as planned.

"Esme?"

She turns and looks into the face of that handsome beach hunk Emma met. *Shit, what's his name?*

Smiling, Esme extends her hand. "Yes, hi, how are you? I hope you're enjoying the wedding." *What the hell is this guy's name?*

He holds her hand for a slight second longer than she likes and says, "Yeah, the wedding is great, as long as I do what the bride says. I'm Ben, by the way. We've met through."

"Yes, of course. You were with Emma at the beach bar.

Nice to see you. You all look quite handsome." *Jesus, I sound like my mother.*

A smile spreads across his face, causing his green eyes to crinkle in a very sexy way. "Well, thank you. I had nothing to do with our wardrobe." He leans in and whispers, "It's all the bride's doing."

Ben's unsettlingly confident demeanor, with his unwavering gaze and dazzling smile, catches Esme off guard—a stark contrast to her usual confident reactions. Taking a moment to gather her thoughts, she delicately runs her well-manicured nails through her silky curls.

"That's the bride's job. She's allowed to boss everyone around, but once that bouquet is tossed, it's all over—back to normal, you might say." Esme flashes her perfect, ruby-red-lipped smile. She is about to say goodbye, but Ben stops her.

"Any chance Emma might be hiding around here somewhere? I would love to see her." *Oh, Emma's hiding alright, under the bedcovers.* "No, why would she be here?"

"A guy can hope, right? I'm here for another few days and I hope to get the chance to get to know her better. I don't have her number; can I share my contact information for you to pass it along to her?"

This fake smile is getting tiresome, but just a bit longer and I'll be back at the cottage.

"Sure, give me your number and I'll make sure she gets it."

"Promise? I know I sound desperate, but I don't want to miss the chance to see her again."

Well, you do sound desperate. "Yup, I promise. Now, I

need to get back to overseeing things, making sure everything runs smoothly—and that the bride and groom are having fun! You too, I hope. Bye-bye."

I sounded like an idiot, like a nervous ninny with a crush. Something about this guy makes me uncomfortable. Esme surveys the scene. The wedding cake has been cut and passed around. *Things should wind down soon, but not soon enough for me.*

Chapter Nineteen

"Friends give you a shoulder to cry on. But best friends are ready with a shovel to hurt the person that made you cry." – Unknown

Secrets

Esme pulls the Audi into the Callahan's drive, top-down, Prince blaring on the sound system. She smiles, thinking back to how many times she has done this. This place, this beautiful piece of property overlooking the ocean, is her safe place. This was the home she would run away to. Here, she was always welcomed, whether she was going through her chubby stage or when she wanted to rip the braces off her teeth and pop every pimple on her face. The Callahans always accepted Esme, even when her own mother wouldn't. Mo strolls over to the car, shading her eyes from the sun.

"Is everyone alive?" Esme asks, stepping out of the car.

"If you mean after last night, yes. Well, barely. Emma is a bit rough around the edges.

She's been in the water a lot today. I swear the ocean is the best hangover cure."

"No truer words have been spoken, Maureen Callahan. Are they at the cottage?"

"Yeah, they are hanging out on the porch, Delle just left."

"Delle? Hmm, wonder what he was doing here?"

Mo shrugs her shoulders. "Maybe picking up the pieces?" She heads back toward her parents' home.

Esme walks through the back screen door of the cottage, kicks off her sneakers, and drops her Hermes purse on the floor.

"Honey, I'm home."

"We're out here."

She walks through the kitchen toward the front porch, noticing a bottle of Patrón on the counter.

Ellenor and Emma are on the old wicker couch facing the ocean. Ellenor's bare feet are propped on the driftwood coffee table, and Emma has her long tan legs flung over Ellenor, resting against the overstuffed pillows from her bed.

"How'd it go?" Ellenor asks, yawning.

"It was fine. Everything went precisely as it was supposed to. Just the way I like it—no surprises. How are you guys doing?" She leans down and kisses Emma on the top of her head. "I'm glad to see you are among the living today. I know you said you don't want to talk about it, but one of these days, you're going to need to come to grips with what Ethan said last night. Not now, though. It's been an exhausting day."

She squeezes Emma's bony shoulder and continues, "Have you thought about dinner? I guess we could go out, or maybe we can order a pizza. I'll pick it up."

Emma moves her legs off of Ellenor and swings around to look at Esme. "I am alive, so I guess I'm doing okay. I do have one thing that I need to say about last night, other than thank you guys for having my back and getting me home. Ellenor told me I gave our Uber driver a hard time just because he was a guy. Jesus, that was unnecessary."

"We tipped him very well, so don't give it another thought." Esme sits on the edge of the coffee table.

"Well, I think I had an excuse. It was surreal seeing Ethan. I struggled to even look at him. I felt like I was stark raving mad. I've loved him since he was a sixteen-year-old boy who lived to surf and who loved me. He used to joke he didn't know which he loved more, me or the waves. I guess he didn't love either. We can dissect this more, but not now. I'm still hungover and revisiting last night, reliving that time is exactly what I do not want to do tonight. There's a roast chicken and potato salad in the fridge. But we can do pizza if you want."

"Nice way to change the subject, Emma. Who cooked a chicken? I can't imagine either of you doing that today—no offense."

"Delle brought it over with the tequila."

Esme looks at Emma, raising her perfectly sculpted eyebrows ever so slightly. "Delle brought dinner and tequila? Why? Why would Delle do that?"

"He brought our bikes back from the Pequod and grabbed the bottle of Patrón when we left. He's very discreet that way." Emma is smiling.

"Okay, chicken, potato salad, and tequila. Sounds like

we have a plan." Ellenor gets up and stretches. "But I'm starting with wine. I'm not sure I can handle any more tequila."

During dinner, they talk about the wedding, Esme sharing every detail from the bride's dress to the couple's signature cocktail. "Oh, that beach hunk was there. He asked about you."

Emma beams, sitting up straight. "He did? What did he say?"

"He wants to see you before he heads off the Cape for home. Wherever that is. Emma, I see that look on your face. Let's google him before you marry him."

"Ben Maloney, thirty-eight years old, single, Vanderbilt graduate." Apparently sensing questions, Ellenor says, "It doesn't say if he was ever married or has kids. But, oh, look, he has a dog."

"That looks like a Chihuahua, but it's kinda cute." Emma moves closer to the screen. "He's an investment broker, lives in Hoboken, and likes photography, sailing, hiking, and rugby."

"Well, he doesn't sound like a serial killer. Here's his contact info." Esme shrugs her shoulders and takes a sip of wine. "I guess the ball's in your court." She raises her wine glass to Emma, giving her a nod of approval.

After dinner, Esme volunteers to clean up the dishes. The cottage has no dishwasher, so she fills the white enamel sink with hot, soapy water and washes each dish carefully before rinsing it under the hot tap and placing it in the drying rack. She thinks about how many times she has been in this kitchen, nostalgia filling her with the familiar warmth one senses when they know they are where they're supposed to be. She dries her hands on the red-and-white-checked dish towel and places it on the old granite counter-top, running her hand along its edge before stepping back outside. She stops in the doorway to take in the scene. Her best friends sit on the old porch, just like they used to. She can hear the waves crashing into the shore in the background, mixed with Ellenor's telltale laugh, and she can smell the subtle scent of Emma's body oil. *This is how life should always be.*

"I have a question." Esme says, adjusting the pillows on the old Adirondack chair before sitting down.

"Shoot," says Ellenor.

"Aside from the issue with the land, what's going on with your brothers? I was surprised to see Delle and Red last night. What were they doing with Ethan? He and Delle seemed tight. I didn't think they stayed in touch after Ethan left. And why would Delle bring over dinner and the tequila? I feel like he's up to something, besides being a loser."

"Jesus Esme, that's harsh, even for you. I already told you he brought our bikes back.

By the way, his business is booming. He bought the William's cottage on Nauset Heights Road a couple of years ago, and he's been doing a great job fixing it up. That does not sound like a loser to me." Emma's voice is tight with irritation.

"He bought that dump? Figures." Esme pours herself more wine, her hand shaking.

"It's not a dump anymore. He's put a lot of work into it. It's all insulated, with new plumbing and wiring. Remember the old front porch that was falling off? It's gone, so the front of the house has a beautiful view of the sunrise over Nauset. I guess you guys are almost neighbors, Esme. The snooty Nauset Heights let a local move in." Emma smirks.

Esme shrugs her shoulders and wrinkles her nose. "Whatever. But good for Delle, I guess."

"Has Delle done something to piss you off?"

"No, I'm just surprised to hear about his one-eighty into a responsible adult. Let's move on." Esme says, unconsciously tapping her foot on the floor.

"Hold on, how do you know more about my brother than me?"

Ellenor and Esme's curious gazes fixate on Emma.

"I ran into Delle my first day back here, and he invited me over to see the house. He's kept in touch, and it was nice to catch up with him."

Esme stops tapping her foot and adjusts in the chair, sitting up straighter. "Delle has been keeping in touch with you? For how long?" She takes a large sip of wine.

"I'm not sure, but for a while. Not a big deal. So, as I started to say, when I told my dad about my visit, he said Delle is becoming something of a celebrity around here. He worked on Skip Appleton's boat for a few years, starting out as a deckhand, eventually moving up to a first mate. And that's how he learned to 'read the water.' Skip taught him about the migration patterns of tuna, bass, and bluefish. Then he learned about watching the changes in the water temperature with the tidal flows and what the birds are doing out over the water. All of this taught him what equipment he should use and when. His little charter business grew to three boats once word got out that the fish just jump in his boat. I think Delle might have started that rumor himself." Emma gives a little laugh and sits back in her chair.

"I had no idea my brother was following in our father's footsteps and doing it much better than him. Very interesting, very interesting indeed."

"Emma, it sounds like you know a lot more about Delle than you're letting on."

"And Esme, it sounds to me like you are jealous."

"Don't be an ass, Emma. What in the world would I have to be jealous about, anyway? But while we seem to still be on the subject of Ellenor's brother, I'd like to know why nobody in your family has ever married. Except for your parents, of course. Any ideas, Ellenor?"

"That's easy—my bonehead brothers are Neanderthals. No woman in their right mind would look at them twice."

"I think they are all damn good-looking. Except for OJ, of course." Emma pipes up.

"Okay, so that's your brothers' reason, and by the way, it does sound like Delle has turned things around. I'm happy for him. But what about you, Ell? Esme and I have talked about it and wonder why you haven't been in an actual relationship, ever."

"You and Esme talk about me behind my back? God, you guys, that makes me feel awful."

Esme waves her hand in the air as if to swat away a fly. "Oh, Ellenor, it's not like we've never done it. I mean, it seemed like all you and I did was talk every night when Emma was going through her own personal hell."

Emma looks up from picking at her fingernail. "You guys talked about me? Why would you do that?"

"Because you were drowning, and we were doing our best to keep you afloat. We needed to talk strategy, plan Ethan's murder, and get you back on dry land. Mostly, we talked about how to murder Ethan." A wide grin spreads across Ellenor's face, revealing her flawlessly white teeth.

"Okay, let's return to the conversation about the wayward Snow family and their issues with relationships."

Emma continues. "We've talked about you too, Esme." She has a smug, taunting look on her face.

"What or why would you guys talk about me? Other than how successful I am and that I'm living the all-American dream?" Esme flips a curl over her shoulder, taking on an air of superiority.

"Knock it off, Esme. We all know you aren't happy, and we will probably talk about you tonight if you go to bed first."

"No, seriously, what did you guys say about me?"

"It's ancient history."

"Tell me."

"Okay, Ell and I talked about how we wanted to help you when you got pregnant right before graduation. We didn't know what to do—you seemed so vulnerable, which isn't you at all. But we were all just kids ourselves, and it was a shock to find out that one of us was going to have a baby."

Esme softens. "I'm sorry. I know I seemed to disappear from you and almost everyone else back then, but knowing you were there if I needed you helped me get through that time. Whether or not you know it, that's what kept me going. So, if you talked behind my back, I know it was out of love. That's the same for all of us. If one of us is in trouble, the other two need to figure out how to help. Oh, Ell and I are still working on Ethan's murder, just in case you're wondering."

Esme stops for a sip as a gentle summer breeze slips onto the porch, carrying the smell of salt air and washing away the building tension.

Never one to let anything go, Esme asks, "Can we please get back to the beginning of this conversation, to the Snow family's lack of relationships? And Ellenor, while we are on the subject, didn't you say you met someone but weren't ready to talk about it?" With a determined glint in her eyes, she leans back in her chair, waiting for Ellenor to respond.

Ellenor remains quiet, looking out toward the ocean. These are her people, this is her safe space, yet she hesitates. The words are right there, ready to burst from her lips. But they don't.

"Ell, this isn't an inquisition. I'm sorry if we've upset you," Emma whispers.

The porch is silent except for the piercing squawks of seagulls overhead riding the breeze toward the ocean.

"I did meet someone kind of special," Ellenor says softly.

Esme jumps up from the wicker chair, spilling her wine. "Ellenor Louise Snow, what the hell? You tell us everything right this minute. Name, age, and occupation."

"My middle name isn't Louise," Ellenor says, looking at Esme as if she's gone off the deep end.

Esme tries to wipe the spilled wine off the table with the sleeve of her shirt as she says, "Yes, I know you don't have a middle name. I got carried away—can you blame me? But I do think Louise would be a lovely middle name for you."

Ellenor keeps her gaze out to the ocean. *How do I do this? How do I say what I think is true? What if they hate me? What if I ruin everything? Maybe I should just make something up. I met a guy. I like him. Then next week I'll say he drowned in the Black Sea.*

Emma slides closer to her, gently saying, "Ell, you know we love you, and whatever you have to say, no matter how hard it is for you to get it out, Esme and I will always, always love you. So if you want to tell us about it, go for it. And if you aren't ready, that's okay too." She squeezes Ellenor's hand while Esme sits across from her with her eyes wide open and her lips glued together.

"Okay, but we need shots before I tell you what's going on." She takes a deep breath to try to calm herself, but her stomach is churning and her heart racing.

"Here we go, last night's Patrón, lime, and salt." Esme sets the tray down on the weathered table and pours three shots, handing one to each of her friends. "Can we skip the salt and lime and just dive right into this?"

"Yes," they say in unison then down the cold clear liquid in one gulp.

"Okay, before I do this, promise you won't interrupt me until I'm done. So no questions or comments, got it?"

"Yes."

"One more shot, and I will spill my guts to you."

The only sound on the porch is the soft sound of wind chimes in the breeze. It seems even the seagulls have stopped to listen.

"You guys know that I've had plenty of relationships." She sees Esme look at her skeptically. "Alright, maybe not actual relationships, but I've had my share of more-than-one-night stands. Look at Charley—he and I have been seeing each other for a while now. "Seriously? Charley?" Esme interrupts with obvious disdain for Ellenor's on-again, off-again hookup.

"Shhh, let her finish."

"It's not Charley, and you promised not to interrupt." Ellenor takes another deep breath, grateful the tequila is giving her some courage. "I've known this person for years. We're friends, sometimes enemies, but mostly friends. Recently, we both discovered an unexpected and powerful attraction toward each other. It's tricky, because our friendship and our day-to-day interactions are very important to us, and we don't want to screw that up with a friends-with-benefits thing. We, or at least I, am too damn old for that. We're both serious about seeing where this goes. And I think it might go far."

Ellenor stops talking to take a deep inhale, and on the exhale, she says, "It's Maggie."

"Maggie? Maggie who?" Esme is confused. "Maggie?"

"Maggie O'Hare. You guys have met her."

Esme stares at Ellenor in disbelief. "Your publisher?"

"She's my agent—there's a difference."

Esme waves her hand in the air again saying, "Whatever, Ellenor. Agent, publisher. It's Maggie?"

"Yup." *I think I might hurl.*

The three women, bonded since childhood, sit together in silence, their shared past woven into the fabric of their being.

Ellenor knows this is big. *Bigger than Esme's pregnancy, bigger than Ethan destroying Emma by running away with a Swedish nanny. This is really, really big.*

Ellenor is looking at Esme and Emma, wondering what they're going to say, what they are thinking. She wants to run, run, run to the beach, to dive into the waves, and for the current to take her down swiftly so she doesn't suffer or struggle. Because at this very moment, Ellenor is suffering. She is struggling. She just said she has feelings for a woman, and her confession is being met with silence. *Is this their answer? Disapproving silence?* But it doesn't take long before her friends' words fill the space.

Emma pours them another shot of tequila. *The good thing about very expensive tequila is the buzz hits you slowly, taking you in like a spider to its web, and then the next morning you wish you were dead.*

"Okay," Emma says, "we need more details. How did this happen? When did you start to feel like, I don't know"—she shrugs her shoulders —"like you were, like you are attracted to women? Did you guys have sex already?"

"Emma," snaps Esme. "Stop. We never asked you about

that with Ethan, so why do you think asking Ellenor about Maggie is okay?" She looks back to Ellenor. "But did you?"

Ellenor is grateful for the tequila's liquid courage. With a deep breath and her head down, she mumbles, "Not completely."

"Ell, we aren't looking for those details—unless, of course, you want to share them with us." Esme has a grin on her face as she continues, "It would be nice if at least one of us was having sex. I, for one, would like to know what happened."

"Can you at least let us know how you and Maggie went from a professional relationship to whatever it is now?" Emma asks.

"It's all Jill's fault, although in hindsight, I probably need to send her some kind of gift basket or something."

"Who's Jill?"

"Jill is my handler. But only when I'm on the road."

Esme grabs the bottle of tequila but then seems to think better of pouring more shots. They probably all want to be as clear-headed as possible for this conversation.

Instead, she says, "You have a handler? What the hell does that mean?"

"It means I can't be trusted. I'm not responsible. I drink too much, and I have a tendency to let loose after I stand in front of a group of strangers, pouring out my heart and soul, talking about my books. Even though my stories are fiction, people want to press me to say the things I write about are things that happened to me." Ellenor runs her hand through her hair, causing her cowlick to appear, just like it did when she was a kid. She gets off the couch and starts toward the kitchen door as she says in a tiny voice, "I lost it in Nantucket, and Jill called Maggie."

"Don't leave. It's okay, Ell. You can tell us," Emma says.

She shakes her head in defeat, sitting back down. "I kind of freaked when we flew over the Cape going to Nantucket. Jill thought it was because of the turbulence in that tiny plane, but that wasn't it. It was the stress of knowing I was so damn close to home, and that made me want to punch the pilot in the face, grab the wheel, and down the plane. I felt like I was suffocating, claustrophobic or something. I didn't even realize I was gripping Jill's arm. Poor kid."

"You didn't try to punch the pilot, did you?"

"No, Esme, I didn't try to punch the pilot, tempting as it was."

"Well, it's obvious the plane landed safely, for which we are all grateful," Esme says. "So, then what? Where does Maggie fit in here?"

"Yup, we landed. The pilot never knew what was happening behind him. A car was waiting for us. All I had to do was get off the plane, walk over to the car on the tarmac, and climb in. That's all I had to do. Jill waited outside for our luggage. I didn't need to do one damn thing, but I did."

Ellenor put her head in her hands and continued. "That's when I gave the driver a hundred bucks and asked him to discreetly deliver a handle of Tito's to the inn after he dropped us off. And he did. And I proceeded to get rip-roaring drunk."

"But why? I don't understand. You love it here. I know

you do. Why would coming home send you off the deep end?"

"I love this," Ellenor says, her arms outstretched, encompassing the screened-in porch, the sprawling lawn, and the mesmerizing view of the beach leading to the vastness of the ocean. "I love this place, your family, you guys. I love this, not what I grew up with." Her voice cracks with emotion.

"So, Maggie? Can we get back to her?"

"Right, Maggie. Jill called her. She told her about my meltdown on the plane, and she saw the driver deliver the vodka. Maggie told me that Jill was worried I was having a nervous breakdown and that she couldn't help me by herself. Maggie got the very next flight out to Boston."

"Go on." Esme is clearly holding back. She's known Ellenor since they were five years old—Ellenor doesn't like to be pushed.

"Maggie got to the inn the next morning, really early. I was out cold—I think I was still drunk. She assessed the situation, in true Maggie style, and took over. She wasn't mad, but she was adamant that I needed to get my act together. I just wanted to vomit and go back to bed. She made me get up and take a shower. I could barely stand up. Maggie got in the shower with me, in her underwear, and washed my hair, scrubbed me so hard I thought I would scream. Then she turned the water to ice cold, jumping out before it hit her. That's when I did scream—and curse— then I started laughing. The situation was absurd. She was standing there, soaking wet in her underwear and handing me a towel, and then she started laughing. Once that happened, we couldn't stop. Oh my God, you guys, it was what the doctor ordered—laughter, and someone to pick me up when I had hit the bottom. We dried off and put on those fancy white robes that high-end places always have in the room. You guys know what I'm talking about, the kind you want to steal?"

"Yes, we all know about those stupid robes—continue," Esme says through clenched teeth.

"Right, of course you do. Maggie ordered us room service, and she stopped being Maggie, my agent. We sat on the bed and she gently towel-dried my hair. She asked questions, and I answered them. Somehow her questions, and maybe Maggie herself, pushed me to open up. I told her everything about my childhood. How confusing it was to love and hate a place at the same time. It wasn't as hard as I thought it would be to talk about how ashamed I am of my family. Maggie didn't say anything. She quietly sipped her coffee and listened to me—she really listened."

Emma curls her feet under her and straightens a pillow on the wicker couch. "I don't understand. Why are you ashamed of your family? Esme and I loved being at your house. I know your brothers were a pain in the ass, but so were my sisters. I felt like a wild child there—*Lord of the Flies*, without the drama."

"What you guys don't seem to understand is that I knew we were poor, really poor. People roll their eyes when I say I grew up eating lobster. The only reason for that is because sometimes that was all my father would bring home after days away fishing and hauling in his lobster traps. What he couldn't sell, we ate. My mother would bring leftovers from the restaurant if she could. When I was young, I thought everyone was like us. And then I learned we weren't like everyone else I knew."

Ellenor turns to face Emma. "I was around five when I started noticing the differences. You had—and still have—warm, loving parents and sisters who teased you but adored you. The love I sensed from your parents toward each other and their kids opened my eyes to how a true family is supposed to be. My father was a relentless, self-righteous bully. His behavior toward my mother was nothing short of demeaning, and he took pleasure in belittling my brothers. He paid no attention to me, which in hindsight, is probably a blessing. And the kicker out of all of this is he had a reputation of being a lousy fisherman, she was just a waitress at the worst place in town, and everyone knew it."

"Ellenor, I think we're getting off-topic here. I understand you had some genuine issues with your family. I think almost everyone has family issues," Esme says. "I grew up thinking my father abandoned me and blamed him for everything wrong in my life. When I was old enough to confront him, I discovered that my mother had been lying about what happened between them. She is at the top of the list when I get back into therapy. Now, can we please get back to Maggie? How did it go from agent to lover?"

Ellenor shakes her head and covers her eyes. "I need a cigarette."

"Okay, let's pack our beach bags, take the tequila, and go down to the beach. We just need to be sober enough to get back up those stairs. We aren't as young and agile as we used to be."

With the sun dipping below the horizon, casting long shadows and painting the sand with soft, golden light, they lay their beach blanket on the sand, still warm from the afternoon sun. Ellenor puts out her cigarette, stands up, and undresses. "The tide's going out, the moon is rising, and this is the perfect time to go in. I'm doing it only to get through this soul-bearing revelation. The ocean cures everything. Care to join me?"

With no hesitation, they strip naked and run to the water's edge, dropping towels before they race into the water. It's cold, invigorating, and soothing at the same time. A comfort to each of them. Ellenor dives under each wave with skill and grace, blocking out the world.

Emma floats out beyond the waves, her mind adrift. Esme body surfs, crashing into the shore. Each wave hurls her beneath the water, spinning her in every direction, yet she resurfaces every time, seemingly driven by sheer determination to confront the next wave. They come out laughing, falling into each other, and holding each other up. Back at the beach blanket, now in hoodies and cozy sweats, Esme pours them each a shot.

She holds up her solo cup and says, "Promise—no drunk swimming, no matter what. I'm sure you remember what happened last time."

"Yes ma'am, no drunk swimming," says Ellenor with a twinkle in her eyes.

"Not to worry. That was so embarrassing," Emma says then downs her shot. "Now, can we get back to the conversation?"

Ellenor lights another cigarette, and exhales, saying,

"I'm not sure what more there is to say. We're exploring our feelings, testing the water, you might say."

"How much water have you tested?"

"We're getting to know each other even though we know each other. There's a lot more to each of us that we don't know. You guys must know what I mean."

"No Ellenor, I don't know. The last thing you said was you and Maggie were sitting on the bed in robes, having breakfast while you poured out your heart and soul to her. You told her things you've never told us. So, keep going—what happened next?"

"If I didn't know better, I'd say you sound jealous, Esme."

"Maybe I am jealous, or maybe I'm hurt. I don't understand how you can tell a perfect stranger things that you never told Emma and me." Esme stands up defiantly and kicks a clam shell, clearly fighting back tears.

"Sit down, please. I don't know why I never talked to you guys about how I felt. Sometimes it's easier to talk to strangers about hard things. Maggie isn't a stranger, but I felt a powerful compulsion to share that stuff with her. Jesus, I thought you'd be angry with me for telling you about Maggie, not for what I told her." She grinds her cigarette butt into the sand and puts it in her hoodie pocket.

"We would never be mad at you, no matter what your choices are. I think Esme's reaction is proof of that. Uncalled for, but it shows us that our bond is something that we maybe take for granted. Maybe we all keep some things to ourselves. But that doesn't minimize our love for each other."

Esme sits down and hugs Ellenor. "Emma's right, as usual. I'm sorry. So, let's finish this story. Where are you and Maggie now? What else happened in Nantucket?"

"Not much. We walked around town. I brought her to Mitchell's bookstore. She took pictures of me holding my newest release, which was embarrassing. We checked out some boutiques and art galleries and had lunch at the Brotherhood. I walked her to the ferry, and off she went, back to San Francisco. I went back to the inn and focused on my book talk. Jill and I walked over to the atheneum, where the author's talks were being held. I got to meet some amazing local authors. I had forgotten what an impressive building the atheneum is. It's almost intimidating, but I didn't let that sneak into my head. At seven, it was my turn to talk, and I did it. And I did it with no alcohol. But in alcohol's defense, I drank so much the night before that I think I would have puked if I drank—water was my beverage of choice. Sparkling water, because, after all, it was Nantucket. I feel good about how the presentation went, and Jill agreed. I didn't meet Oprah, but who knows what will come of this book tour? The end."

"What's that supposed to mean—the end?"

"The end of the tour. That's all," Ellenor says, shrugging her shoulders. She smiles smugly and leans back on her elbows. "Oh, you want to know more about me and Maggie?"

A resounding yes is the response.

Ellenor smiles. *Yes, my friends do love me for who I am,*

no matter what. "Like I said, she went back, and now I'm here. We decided to chill until I get back to the city and then reassess. I want to take it slow—this is a big step, and I don't want to rush into anything or screw up anything."

"Sounds like a plan," Esme says. "Let's get back to the cottage before we drink anymore and can't make it up all thirty-seven of those damn stairs. But first I have a question. How long can we stay?"

Chapter Twenty

"I am who I am today because of the choices I
made yesterday." — Eleanor Roosevelt

Esme

E sme winces and opens one eye. The sun is streaming
in on her, announcing that she will not be sleeping in
today. She pulls the patchwork quilt over her head, waiting
for the throbbing headache to make its usual morning
appearance. Instead, she feels surprisingly refreshed. Mrs. C
always said the salt air could make anyone sleep like a baby.
She slips out of bed, in a gray tank top and black boxers,
and tiptoes barefoot across the bedroom floor. The house is
quiet as she measures out the coffee and sets it to brew.
Esme gazes out the kitchen window, looking past the lawn
and out to the ocean, captivated by its beauty. *It's different
every day.* She pours the steaming hot coffee into her mug,
taking in its deep aroma, then steps out into the backyard.
She tilts her face to the sky, feeling the warmth of the
morning sun on her skin. *Am I really going to go through*

with this idea? *I should just stay here. But that's what I always do—stay in line, don't make waves.* She shakes her head of unruly curls and walks back into the house and toward her bedroom to decide what to wear on this ill-advised adventure. Esme's clothes are neatly folded in the old wooden bureau and hung in the matching armoire. She starts with the hanging clothes, all designer labels, and all too much for the effect she hopes to achieve. Next, she tries the folded clothes and winds up pulling them out of the drawers and tossing them onto her unmade bed. She surveys the damage. *I never thought my room would look like Ellenor's. What a disaster. I wish I could be the person who feels confident to just throw on a simple white T-shirt and cut-off jeans without a second thought, like Ell and Emma, But I don't have that confidence.* After much deliberation, she decides on a white eyelet mini dress with spaghetti straps, puts it on, and takes in her reflection in the full-length mirror. Judgment rears its ugly head. *My curls are out of control this morning, but I kind of like it—they have a casual, beachy vibe. Exactly the look I'm going for. I look okay—not fat, but not thin. My arms are still firm, and my legs look okay. A little tan does wonders, that's what Mom used to say. It is what it is. I don't have a lot to work with.*

After brushing her teeth and applying the obligatory sunscreen, she gives herself one last glance in the mirror before heading out. Slipping out the front door, she feels the warmth of the sun on her skin and the cool grass beneath her bare feet. Esme finds her flip-flops in the back seat of the Audi and walks down the beach toward 51 Nauset Heights Road—toward Delle Snow. She walks with purpose along the shoreline until she comes to the long set of stairs with a sign posted. Private. Nauset Heights Residents Only. No Trespassing. She climbs all twenty-two steps, just as she did when she was a kid. Only this time, Esme is winded at the top. Without a chance to think twice about what she's doing, Esme walks through the neighborhood and stops when she comes to Delle's house. She smiles, admiring the transformation of what was once the Heights' worst cottage into a charming Cape Cod-style home.

"Esme?"

She whips around at the sound of her name to find Delle standing behind her.

"Delle, what are you doing here?" she asks, twisting her wedding rings on her finger, betraying her attempt to be casual.

Delle is standing in front of her, juggling his clamming gear and shifting his tall, lean body from one bare foot to the other, his gaze locked on Esme. His eyes resemble Ellenor's—a mesmerizing mix of blue and gray, reminding Esme of the sea.

"I live here." He smirks, glancing toward his house. "What about you?"

"I was going to my mother's house and guess I got turned around and wound up here. There've been a lot of changes to the Heights." She shades her eyes with her hand, looking around as if to give her words validation.

"Not that many, Es." His tone softens. "But you're here, so do you want some coffee? Still drink it black?"

"Got a beer?"

Delle tips his head towards his right shoulder and chuckles. "Ah, a breakfast beer. Rough night last night?"

"Not so bad, but we finished off the bottle of Patrón you brought over. Thanks, I guess. Oh, and rumor has it you're responsible for feeding us last night. Again, thank you. But I'm curious, why did you go to all that trouble?"

"No trouble at all. Now, let me go grab those beers." Esme watches as Delle walks away. He is so familiar to her, even twenty years later. Same old outfit, a T-shirt and jeans, even on a hot summer day. Barefoot, as usual, tan, as usual, and the same mop of blond hair he's had for as long as she has known him. She notices Delle is more muscular than he was when they were teenagers. *It looks good on him. He's aging well, unlike me.* Esme consciously sucks in her stomach and stands up straight. Shoulders back, as her mother would say. She wanders to the backyard and spots a dingy lying on the grass. Esme smiles and runs her hand over the boat—"My Girl" is still clearly painted on its side. She goes back in time to when they were all teenagers. She remembers when Delle bought this dingy, she remembers when he named it *My Girl*, and she remembers kissing him. The first kiss they shared left an enduring mark etched in her very being.

"There you are," Delle says, handing her a bottle of Summer Ale. "I see you found *My Girl*."

"Thanks." She accepts the ice-cold beer, puts it to her lips, and takes a long, cold swallow. "She looks good."

Delle smiles at Esme, takes a swig of beer, and in a playful voice says, "She sure does."

Esme begins to feel uncomfortable. His smile is intoxicating. *What am I doing here?* Spurred by the beer on an empty stomach, Esme turns her back to Delle, looking out to his own perfect view of the inlet. "Delle, are you and Emma seeing each other?"

He walks over to stand beside her. "Why on earth would you ask me that, Es?"

"I saw the look between you two at the Pequod the other night. She looked at you before she told Ethan to start talking. Why would she do that? And I didn't know you and Ethan were still friends."

Her questions are met with silence. *Shit, have I crossed the line?*

"Not that it's any of your business, but Ethan and I are still in touch. We try to get together once or twice when he's back on the Cape. And as far as your question about Emma goes, you should ask her. You guys have always been super tight—why ask me?"

"Ah, so you're telling me you're a kiss-and-don't-tell kinda guy?"

Delle raises an eyebrow and with a biting laugh says, "You of all people should know I'm definitely not a kiss-and-don't-tell kinda guy."

Esme takes another sip of her beer, tears forming in her eyes. She doesn't look at him. "I don't know why I'm asking you any of this. I don't even know why I'm here. I don't know anything anymore." Her tears come, streaming down her face. *There is no going back now.* Delle gently takes the beer from her and sets it on the grass next to his. He turns

Esme toward him, delicately brushes away a tear, and pulls her into a warm, comforting embrace. She sobs into his T-shirt while he strokes her curls and murmurs into her ear, "It's okay, Es, it's okay.

Wiping away her tears, Esme takes a deep breath and steps away from Delle. "Sorry, I don't know what got into me. God, I'm so embarrassed." She says, wiping her nose with the back of her hand. "You must think I'm crazy. Well, maybe I am, just a little bit." Despite her best efforts, her smile is forced, barely concealing the considerable storm of emotions bubbling at the surface.

He doesn't look at her. Instead, Delle focuses on what is safe for him—the ocean. "You've always been a little crazed. That's what I love about you." He turns to look at her. "Why are you here, Esme? I know you didn't just get turned around in the neighborhood. I know you didn't come here to ask me about Emma. Esme, we made a pact. Well, you made the pact, and I've done what you asked. I've stayed away from you. That's what you wanted, and that's what I've done. And now you're here, crying in my yard?" He grabs her shoulders and looks straight into her big brown eyes. "What do you want from me, Esme?"

"I can't tell you why I'm here. I don't know why I'm here. And if I let myself think about what I want, even for a second, I might drown."

"Come on, let's sit over at the firepit, where we'll have some privacy. I don't need these nosey Nauset Heights neighbors spreading any rumors about me."

His attempt at humor is lost on Esme. Her eyes dart around. *What if someone does see us?* She follows Delle to the back of his yard where the round concrete firepit sits on a patio of faded red bricks on the edge of a cliff overlooking the inlet. Esme sinks into the deep, plush cushions of the U-shaped teak sectional, admiring the large elevated wooden planter boxes brimming with vegetables and bright-colored flowers that create a secluded and intimate patio space. Esme is impressed, surprised, and a little proud of what Delle has created hidden in his backyard.

"This is beautiful, Delle," she says, taking it all in. "Did you do this all yourself?"

Delle sits down next to Esme. "Yeah, I laid the patio brick and built the fire pit the first year I was here. Last summer I added the planters. Who knew I had a green thumb? I guess I get that from my mother."

Leaning back in his seat, Delle turns to face Esme, a relaxed smile crossing his face. "Now tell me again why I found you standing in front of my house?"

Esme nervously twirls a lock of hair around her finger, creating a corkscrew curl when she stops. "Like I said, I don't know why I'm here. Being back at the cottage, hanging out at the beach, and being with Emma and Ellenor has unlocked a lot of things I buried. I've forgotten so much about what life was like when we were teenagers. Now I look back and wonder how I wound up this version of Esme."

"This version looks pretty good to me."

"This version is a mother, a wife, a business owner. Where is the girl who loved to surf?

Where did she go? It's so sad, like a mermaid who came to land to die. That's how I feel. So I came here to feel like I used to. Young, reckless—full of piss and vinegar, as your mother used to say. I came to you to find Esme Prince."

Delle takes a second to look around his yard before moving to sit closer to Esme. "I can't help you recapture your youth. If I found that magic potion, I'd be richer than Jeff Bezos. But I can help you feel a little bit of what you remember about us. Tell you what." He tucks a curl behind her ear. "How about you go over to your mother's house and unlock your bedroom window? I'll be over in about thirty minutes. It'll be just like old times—you, me, and some fun."

As he smiles at her sheepishly, his head tilts, and his eyes sparkle with a mischievous glint. Esme stares at him. The thought of reliving that exciting, forbidden love is tempting. *Do I dare?*

The sound of a screen door slamming breaks the spell. "Delle, baby, I've been looking all over for you." Mary Pembroke steps out of the back door onto the deck. She's barefoot, tan, and in white panties and a white tank top with no bra, revealing every bit of Mary Pembroke, from her clavicles to her ankles. Mary Pembroke, three years ahead of Esme in high school, was the beautiful, popular captain of the cheerleading squad. Everyone wanted to be friends with her. If not friends, everyone knew to stay out of her sight for self-preservation—she was also the queen of the mean girls.

She saunters toward the two of them with a sly smile. Her once-thick, shiny blond hair is brittle and thin. Years of bleaching have taken their toll. Wrinkles now line her deeply tanned face and lips, revealing the consequences of too much sun and smoking.

"Well, well, well, is that little Esme Prince? First Emma Callahan and now Esme. Your baby sister's friends are showing up like rats abandoning a sinking ship."

Esme is caught off guard. Delle rises, but Esme remains seated, emotions overwhelming common sense. *What is she doing here? In her underwear? This bitch took pleasure in torturing Ellenor when we were younger. Why would Delle do this to his sister? And to me?* Esme's not sure what she wants to happen, but the options are running through her mind. *Beat the hell out of her? Or have Delle take me in his arms and passionately kiss me? Perhaps it's best if I simply walk away with my dignity intact.*

Esme rises and tosses her head to either side with a look of innocence and a smile that says *don't fuck with me.*

"Hi, sorry. Do we know each other?"

"Of course we do. What do you have, Alzheimer's or something?"

Delle stays square in the middle of these two women. He is probably not sure what is next, but his money should be on Esme.

"Hmm, nope, I'm pretty sure I would remember you." *Two can play the mean-girl game.*

"Jesus, I'm Mary Pembroke, prom queen, captain of the cheerleading squad." She takes a step closer, but the look on Esme's face stops her in her tracks.

"Wait a minute." Esme gives Mary a not so subtle once over, a fake smile spreading across her face. "Mary Pembroke! Oh my God, it's been so long. Now I remember you. I would never have recognized you. Wow, how many years has it been? I'd say about twenty years, and you're still referring to yourself as the prom queen. That's hysterical. Oh, and I see you're still a sun worshipper and a smoker." Despite her chipper tone, Esme's words cut through the air like knives aimed directly at Mary.

Delle is ready. He's standing his ground—he knows Esme, and this may get out of hand.

Mary Pembroke stumbles on her words and her footing. "Delle, baby, can you make me some coffee? I left my mug on my side of the bed." She smirks at Esme. "Thanks, sweetie."

Esme tosses her curls and smiles her sweetest smile. "The last thing I remember about you is you were working at the fish market after graduation. God, when I graduated, years after you, I was so excited to leave the Cape and move to Boston and get married. What about you? Married? Any kids? I'm here for a quick visit with old friends. Our Beacon Hill apartment is a short drive from here. Perfect for a day trip to check on my Heights house."

She turns her head to Delle and gives him a sexy wink before setting her eyes back on Mary. In a mocking tone, she asks, "Are you here vacationing?"

Before Mary can respond, before Delle can make a move, Esme puts on her tortoise shell Ray Bans, picks up her flip-flops, and walks over to Delle.

"It was great catching up with you. We should do this more often. I'm going to take off now and check on my Heights house. I need to be sure all the windows are locked. Thanks for the breakfast beer." She leans in, kisses Delle on the cheek, leers at Mary, and walks toward where she should have walked in the first place—her mother's house.

She doesn't bother to check on the house. Instead, she walks past it and storms back to the Callahan's, hoping she can get a cigarette from Ellenor. Esme is furious with herself, humiliated, and ashamed. *What the hell is wrong with me?*

Chapter Twenty-One

"It's possible to go on, no matter how impossible it seems." – Nicholas Sparks

Emma

E mma snuggles under her quilt, listening to someone rummaging around the kitchen. *It has to be Esme. Ell would never be up this early.*

The creak of the screen door sparks her curiosity. She plants her tanned feet on the white-washed floorboards and peeks out the window facing the driveway. *Hmm, everyone's cars are here. Maybe Esme is just going for a walk.* Emma considers crawling back into bed, but the aroma of freshly brewed coffee lures her into the kitchen. Reaching for a mug from the overhead cabinet, she sees the note propped against the coffeemaker in Esme's messy handwriting. "Gone for a walk. xoxoxo, Es."

Emma takes her mug of coffee and phone and walks out to the back steps of the cottage. She sits on the weathered top step; her long tan legs are stretched out before her as she takes a moment to breathe in the fresh, salty air and gaze out to the ocean. She checks the time on her phone. *What do I have to lose, other than my dignity? And Ethan took that the day he walked out our front door. Damn, I wish Ell left her cigarettes out in plain sight.*

"Hello?"

"Hi, this is Emma, Emma Callahan. I hope I didn't wake you up." Emma is dying inside. *What the hell am I doing?* She's off the steps, now pacing in the yard. She wants to hurl herself and the phone off the cliff into the ocean below.

"You did wake me up, but I can't think of a nicer way to start my day. Good morning, Emma Callahan."

She stops her nervous pacing and replaces her worried look with a smile. "Good morning to you, Ben Maloney."

The following hour is spent trying on different bathing suits, none of which makes Emma feel confident. She pulls all the clothes out of the old bureau, muttering, "I'm too old to be having a fit about how I look in a bathing suit while sitting around the pool at Chatham Beach Inn." She finally decides on a black one-piece with a plunging neckline and high-cut legs. The look is finished with a simple sleeveless white cotton gauze mid-length cover up. Looking at herself in the full-length mirror, she can't help but smile. She now feels confident, casually cool, and undeniably sexy. Her vintage straw Channel bag and white Espadrille slide sandals complete an outfit made for lounging poolside at the luxury resort.

Ben is waiting for her at the front steps of CBI, and his eyes light up when he sees her approaching. The sight of his irrepressible smile brings Emma's anxiety level from a ten to a seven. An image of Ethan flashes in her mind, but she shakes her head and smiles up at Ben.

"Hi. I'm so glad you're here." He beams, his green eyes sparkling as he reaches his hand out to her.

"Come with me. I reserved a cabana for us as far away from people as possible. And I ordered us a bottle of champagne. I think we should make up for not having a drink together the other day. Oh, wait, that was your fault." He laughs playfully, bumping into her as they make their way across a boardwalk of dark, rich Brazilian wood leading to their cabana. The entire pool area is surrounded by oversized vases and planters of exotic flowers and lush greenery, creating a serene, luxurious ambience. They settle in on the chaise lounges tucked inside the open-air cabana with blue-and-white-striped curtains neatly draped on either side. The small white table between the white mesh loungers holds a bottle of Dom Pérignon chilling in an ice bucket and two flutes.

As Ben pours the champagne, he says, "This is the best I could do since there is no way I can compete with your beautiful beach."

Emma accepts the flute, smiling. "I think you did just fine for a tourist. You said we'd have some privacy, and you've succeeded. This is something I don't experience every day. But where's the wedding crowd? I thought there'd be planned activities to keep you out of trouble." *Damn, I'm flirting with him. This guy brings out the flirt in me.*

"Most of the guests and wedding party have headed back home or are out on their own. The bride and groom left late last night for their honeymoon—their parents are having a small brunch somewhere. I was invited, but…" Ben takes a sip of his champagne, tilts his head, and looks straight into Emma's eyes. "It turns out I had a much nicer offer."

She meets his gaze, and a slow smile spreads across her face as she says, "Seems like a smart choice to me." She sighs contently, placing her sunglasses back on. *This doesn't suck.*

Their conversation has all the classic signs of a first date, despite Emma's internal insistence that it isn't. *It's just two people getting to know each other.*

Ben fills her in on his large family, six older brothers, playing baseball in high school, and how he embraced the freedom of college.

"This may sound corny, but I figured out who I was at Vanderbilt. There wasn't anyone for me to compete against except myself. I relished being on my own and being alone. My roommate had a girlfriend near campus, so he was rarely there. As the youngest of the Maloney boys, college was liberating. My mother still treats me as the baby of the family." He says this with a cynical tone, which Emma picks up on. "But that's enough about me, tell me all about the beautiful Emma Callahan. More champagne?"

Emma thinks for a second before speaking, watching Ben refill her glass. *He's easy to be with and easy to look at, but there's something that I can't figure out yet. Is he overconfident? A spoiled rich kid? Or am I just so uber-aware of looking for red flags? God knows I missed them all with Ethan.* She squeezes her eyes shut to rid herself of any thoughts of Ethan.

"Well, you already know where I come from. I could

just say I grew up on the beach, which I did, but Nauset is so much more than just a beach. It's a land of beauty and magic. A place of awe-inspiring sunsets and sunrises. I witnessed terrifying hurricanes and nor'easters, blistering heat, and destructive winter storms. It was a different time back then—the world, at least my world, was kinder, softer, full of hope and promise. I know, deep in my soul, that growing up where I did profoundly shaped me into who I am today. I will never take that for granted," she says wistfully.

"But enough about where I grew up. The boring truth is, like you, I come from a big family, but it's all girls. My poor father. We drove him up a wall. My mother was the calm one, but she was firm. She would ask questions before coming to any conclusions or deciding what the hell to do with us."

"How so?" Ben sounds genuinely interested.

"Let me think. Oh, here's a good example."

In her best impersonation of her mother, she says, "'Emma, I'd like to discuss last night with you. Have a seat and explain to me why you thought sneaking out in the middle of the night was a smart choice.' That's just one of the many things she put up with from us." Emma smiles at the memories, sipping her champagne.

"She sounds more than reasonable. In fact, I suspect that your wonderful sense of calm and self-assurance are a direct result of your mother's influence and the benefit of growing up where you did. And that's just another reason I feel such a tug toward you."

An awkward silence hangs between them until Emma

blurts out, "I looked up your profile on social media." Her words are a rush of nervous energy.

"What did you think? Did you see anything you liked?"

"Not bad, but there isn't any meat to it. No pictures of Ben as a baby, Ben going to the senior prom, Ben graduating from college. That type of thing."

"I could say the same thing about yours." He laughs.

"Touché." Emma raises her glass, relieved their conversation is back on track.

"Want to jump in the pool? I need to cool off."

Way to change the subject. "Honestly, I'm not a fan of pools. The ocean is just on the other side of the tennis courts. I dare you to jump into the Atlantic Ocean this early in the season."

"Ha, I can handle cold water. I've been known to do a polar plunge once a year or so."

Ben hands Emma one of the blue-and-white-striped beach towels supplied by the resort and tosses his over his broad shoulders. They walk side by side around the back of the tennis courts. As soon as they step onto the sandy white beach, Emma strips off her cover-up and runs straight into the water with no hesitation.

"Come on," she yells, before diving under a wave. *The saltwater is just what I need.* She bobs to the surface. *Two glasses of champagne on an empty stomach, and my self-control goes out with the tide.*

"This was a great idea," Ben says, swimming over to her. "Much better than the pool." They spend the next twenty minutes body surfing, floating, and splashing each other. Emma is in her element—the ocean, her power. They stumble out of the water, holding hands and laughing at each other. Ben picks up a towel and wraps Emma in it. He brushes her wet hair off her face and then tells her she has something in her nose.

"Oh God," Emma says, wiping her nose. "That's embarrassing."

Ben laughs. "I'm hungry, want to get some lunch?" He leans in close to her, water dripping from his thick brown hair. "Maybe some more champagne?"

They lunch on overflowing lobster rolls and Cape Cod potato chips and sip champagne while opening up a bit more about their past.

"The reason my social media pages are dull is that I like it that way. But if you want to know my deep, dark secrets, you're going to have to share yours," he says, just as Emma is about to put a chip in her mouth.

"You first, Ben Maloney—spill your guts," she says playfully.

"I'll skip the fluff on social media. I went to Vanderbilt on a baseball scholarship and graduated with an MBA and an MSFA. After graduation, I stayed in the Nashville area. I wasn't keen on returning home."

"Where's that?"

"I grew up in the middle of nowhere, USA. Landry City, Iowa. Ever heard of it?"

Emma shakes her head.

"I didn't think so," he replies.

Emma catches that cynical tone he used earlier.

"It's near Des Moines, and there's nothing else to say about it. But there was a reason I stayed in Tennessee after graduating. I was dating a girl that I thought was the one for me. You know, the love of your life? I envisioned marriage, kids, and a house anywhere other than where I grew up. I had mapped out my life, and I was ready to jump in with both feet. I asked her to marry me right before graduation, and she accepted. Everyone was so excited. My parents loved Michelle and her parents loved me. Sounds perfect, right?"

Emma nods her head. *Do I want to know what happened? Yes, of course I do.*

"We got an apartment close to campus so Michelle could finish out her last year. The plan was to get married the next summer, right after she graduated. I found a low-level position with a brokerage firm—it was all fine."

"Just fine?"

"Looking back, I realize it was that, just fine. Nothing exciting or challenging. There was no mystery. It was as if I was trying too hard to create what I perceived to be the perfect life."

"What happened?"

Ben pours them more champagne and takes a deep breath. "She ended it three months before the wedding. I came home from work, and she was gone. Her clothes, laptop, everything that was Michelle's. I called her cell, and it went to voice mail. I think I must have called it a thousand times. It was so surreal. I remember my heart racing. I'm sure I was having some kind of panic attack. To be blunt, I wanted to puke. I texted her friends whose numbers I had. Radio silence. I called her parents—the same thing, silence. It was as if Michelle and everything connected to her had disappeared, as if she had never existed. I thought about calling the police, but it was pretty damn obvious she left on her own accord. Finally, I got up my nerve and drove to her parent's house. I was terrified to confirm what I already knew was the truth. I remember parking the car in their driveway, walking up, and knocking on the door. Her dad answered at my first knock, as if he'd been expecting me. He looked as bad as I felt. Long, painful story short, Michelle got cold feet, called off the wedding, and I never heard from her or saw her again."

Emma puts her drink down and leans toward his chair, putting her hand on his bare arm. "Oh my God, Ben, how awful for you, for all of you. And how awful of her. Cold feet or not, you deserved an explanation from Michelle. You were so young, thinking you had it all, ready to conquer the world. I'm so sorry."

Ben runs his hand through his wet hair. "It's ironic that you say that because once I accepted what happened, I quit my job and went home with my tail between my legs. I did a lot of soul-searching and realized I wanted to do exactly that, conquer the world. I needed to move away from my mother's overbearing hovering and figure out my life on my terms. Two of my brothers loaned me some money, and I spent the next ten months in Europe," he says bluntly.

"I don't think that's the end, Ben. How did you wind up in Hoboken?" Emma asks, picking up on his tone again.

"You really did check out my pages, didn't you?" He takes his last sip of champagne and studies the empty glass. "Hoboken is another chapter. That one will have to wait. Your turn."

Emma leans back in the chaise lounge and adjusts her sunglasses. *My turn? How much do I want to reveal to Ben? I'm thinking... not too much. I'm still reeling from seeing Ethan the oth*er *night.*

"My life-altering event may not be drastically different from anyone else's, but when I was going through it, I felt utterly alone, as if I were the only person in the world dying from a shattered heart."

She tucks a strand of hair behind her ear and continues. "I married my high school sweetheart. We had been friends since we were kids, and that friendship grew into what I thought was love. Ethan and I got engaged in college and married in his senior year. He was headhunted and eventually accepted a position with IBM. We packed up our studio apartment, moved to Darrien, Connecticut, bought a house we couldn't afford, and began our life together. I was doing freelance photography and working at a design studio to help pay the bills. That's where I met Grace, another photographer, and we started our own business. Life was good, much better than fine, as you put it. I was happy, in love, and hoped to start a family once Ethan was more established in his career. But all that changed in an instant. I came home one night, Ethan told me he was leaving, and that was that. The rug was pulled out from under me, literally and figuratively. We divorced and sold the house, he went his way, and I went mine. End of story." *There's no need for him to know all the dirty details, such as getting ditched for a younger woman, a Swedish nanny. My life is a cliché, one of those smutty romance novels that aren't the least bit romantic.*

Ben is silent, looking toward the pool. He removes his sunglasses and turns his head to look at her gently before saying, "God, that's terrible. It seems like we have one thing in common."

"What's that?" Emma asks, sensing the heat creep up her neck. She's sure her cheeks are flushed.

"Falling hard for people who were careless with our hearts."

"Yup, it does seem that way." She glances at her watch. *It's time for me to go before things head somewhere I'm not sure about.*

She sits up and swings her long legs to the side of the chaise lounge, facing Ben. "Oh no, I didn't realize the time. I'm sorry, but I need to get going. I've stayed longer than I planned."

Ben sits up and faces her, looking like a kid who just lost his favorite toy. "Really? Do you really need to leave? I was hoping you could stay. We could walk into town for dinner, or better yet, get room service and eat on the terrace. My room has an amazing view of the harbor."

Why is he so handsome, charming, and sexy? Why am I walking away from this? Emma picks up her straw bag, stands up, and says, "That sounds tempting, but I need to get back to the house." She smiles and shrugs her shoulders. "Dinner plans with the family," she lies.

Ben gets up and walks to her. He stands close. "I had hoped you would stay. When are you leaving? I leave tomorrow morning."

"That's still to be determined, but maybe in a day or two. Thanks so much for a wonderful day. It was nice, Ben."

She stands on her tiptoes and gives him a quick peck on his cheek.

"At the very least, let me walk you to your car."

Emma turns, walks away, and with a wave of her arm says, "I'm all set. I know where it is. Thanks again. Bye." *Damn, am I pulling a Michelle, just walking away? Or am I pulling an Ethan?*

Chapter Twenty-Two

"Life moves on and so should we."
— Spencer Johnson

Ellenor

Ellenor is up before everyone for a reason. She's panting, and her toned, tan legs are burning as she runs up the Callahan steps two at a time. She has already gone for a swim and a run on the beach to prepare for her morning meeting with her family. Ellenor needs to be on her A-game for what she is about to do.

The screen door slams behind her as she enters the kitchen. *How many times has that door slammed behind me?* She gives a shallow sigh. She sees Esme's barely legible hand-written note, then checks her phone and sees the text from Emma letting her know she is at CBI. *I think that's where the hunky beach guy is staying. What is our little Emma up to?* She pours a cup of coffee and takes a quick outdoor shower to rinse off the salt water. Ellenor would love to linger under the hot water—showering outside is heaven in her mind—but she's on a schedule and needs to keep moving. She gets dressed in jean shorts, a T-shirt, and her black Converse sneakers. As she pulls one of the old bikes out of the garage, she hesitates for a minute. *Why do I want to get involved? It's not like I'm ever coming back here. Screw it, here goes.* She peddles from the Callahan's to her father's house, surprised that it's not as easy as it once was. *I used to do this ride twice a day, sometimes more, in bare feet. I guess I need to start working out more.* She pedals up to the front of the house and leans her bike against an old pine tree in the yard. She recognizes the three trucks in the driveway—her dad's, Delle's, and Red's. But there's another car pulled off to the side. *Great. I don't need some stranger giving his two cents while I try to plead my case.* She opens the front door.

Ellenor's heart is pounding. "Hello? Anyone here?" The two dogs greet her, tails wagging, as she steps into the house. She bends to pat them. "Jesus, you stink."

"We're out back," someone yells from the deck.

Ellenor takes a minute to glance around the living room where she spent the first eighteen years of her life. *Someone needs to vacuum in here, open up a few windows, and wash these poor old dogs.* She stops at the kitchen sink to rinse her hands, dries them on her shorts, and steps out to the old deck. Sitting around the long picnic table is her family. The Snow boys, as they were once called. She frowns. *Now they're the Snow men.*

Each of her brothers is named after their father, Ordelle, in some form or another. The oldest is Ordelle Junior, OJ for short, next is Delle, and Red is the youngest son. Their parents were running out of names, or more to the point, ways to spell Ordelle differently when Ellenor was born.

After three boys, Ellen Snow was thrilled to finally have a little girl, and she planned to name her after herself, just as her husband had done with all the boys. That didn't fly with Ordelle—he ruled the roost in that house. But Ellen Snow ruled Ordelle when push came to shove. The compromise was Ellenor. Ellen—with the letters *o* and *r* at the end. Ellenor. This was Ellen Snow's way to placate Ordelle. He wasn't thrilled, but he knew when to back down from his wife.

It takes a second for her to realize who came in the car—Ordelle Junior. With a big grin on his face, he stands up. His eyes are twinkling as if he's on the verge of sharing a joke, but OJ never jokes. This smile, along with a nose that has been broken more times than any of them can count, sets OJ apart from the rest of them. He is a dead ringer for Ordelle. His dark brown hair is cut to mimic his father's crew cut, and his deep-set brown eyes share an almost identical intensity. Delle, Red, and Ellenor are the complete opposite of OJ. These three siblings, all with the same profile—Roman nose and high cheekbones—share an uncanny resemblance. There are subtle differences like the shade of their blond hair, their mannerisms, but it's their startling blue-gray eyes that instantly connect them.

OJ smothers Ellenor in a tight bear hug, pulls away, and looks down at her. "Surprised?"

Ellenor takes a step back. "You bet," she says, gritting her teeth.

"It's so good to see you, Ellenor. It's been too long. We need to catch up. How long are you in town for?" He steps closer, towering over her, and gives her a punch to her upper arm.

Momentarily speechless, Ellenor rubs her arm and glares at him.

Aside from having this family meeting, the last thing Ellenor wants to do is spend time alone with OJ. He is full of himself—a condescending bully. Much like her father.

Ellenor quickly recovers from the shock of the punch, pats OJ on the chest, and says, "I'm not sure. Probably leaving tomorrow." Her words are icy cold. She moves away from him and takes a seat on the opposite side of the picnic table.

"Ellenor Snow, your brother has driven all the way from New Bedford. The least you can do is carve out some time to spend with him."

She cringes at her father's harsh tone. *New Bedford is an hour away. I flew across the country, and nobody has made an effort to spend time with me.* She wants to say those thoughts out loud.

"We'll see, but right now I'd like to talk about why I asked that we have this family meeting. I have a plan that might save the property." She fixes her eyes directly on her father. "Please hear me out before you decide anything."

"You have a plan?" OJ snorts.

Experience has taught Ellenor to tread lightly with these four male egos, each one worse than the other.

"It's not my plan. It's Mr. Callahan's." First lie of the day.

"What the hell has George Callahan got to do with anything?" OJ asks.

She clears her throat and sits up straight on the hard wooden bench. "I overheard him talking about how much better he feels now that his property taxes have been lowered." Lie number two.

Delle gets up from the picnic table. "Anybody want a beer?"

"Sure" is the unanimous response, including Ellenor's. She puts her elbows on the old table and runs her hand through her hair, exasperated that he has interrupted her train of thought.

She takes a big swallow of her beer and continues. "It seems the Callahans and almost every year-rounder in town were shocked when the tax bills came out last year. He knew with all the changes happening on the Cape, all the new building and the increase in summer people, the property taxes were undoubtedly going to increase every year and that would hit him hard financially. He'd have to sell. But he found a loophole and went to a land attorney."

"Never heard of that kind of lawyer," OJ growls, smirking at Ellenor.

"I never had either, OJ, but they exist. With the attorney's advice, he put the property, all of it, into what's called a conservation trust," Ellenor says without looking at him. She really wants to pour her beer over his head but knows that would not end well.

"I don't like it already," her father grumbles.

"Dad, let her finish."

Ellenor smiles gratefully at Red and takes another gulp of beer before saying, "The way it works is you sell your property, however much you want, to the Cape Cod

Conservation group. The property is still yours; the only stipulation is that you can't build on it. This way it's deemed a protected open space and stays in the family. There are other incentives, but the big one is a tax break on the land."

Ellenor is met with silence. Her father is the first to respond, putting his large, calloused hands, skin rough and cracked from years of hard work, on the table.

"This sounds like fool's gold to me."

"You got that right, Dad," OJ pipes up, crossing his arms over his chest.

Red speaks quickly, peeling the label off his beer, his words tumbling out of his mouth. "Let's not just say no without looking into it. I've heard of conservation trusts, and we all know the Cape Cod Conservation Commission is here to look out for what's left of our land here. I think we should talk to this attorney that George C. used. It can't hurt."

OJ glares at Red, cracking his knuckles one by one in a slow, deliberate manner. The sound brings back memories of her father doing that—right before he was about to explode. "Ellenor, this sounds like your crazy, left-wing California crap." He turns to his father, ignoring the rest of them. "Dad, you aren't listening to this bullshit, right? It's time to sell the land and move on." He pounds his fist on the table. "Let's be done with it now."

Ellenor jumps at the sound, Red shakes his head, and Delle remains silent. Her father is quiet, looking out toward the ocean.

"I'm not sure about this plan of yours or listening to George Callahan. Your mother made me promise I'd save the land for you kids, but that's getting harder and harder to do. I've got twelve acres left. I was gonna leave each of you an acre. That would leave eight acres, plus this house as some kind of security. If I have to sell off another couple of acres to do that, then that's what I'll do."

Delle's the first to speak. "Dad, I've got my own place, I don't need to take an acre from you. I'm happy in the Heights."

"I thought I'd just keep doing what I'm doing and stay here." Red keeps his head down, not looking at anyone.

"You mean you plan to keep on mooching off Dad—is that right, Red? Solid plan, dude. So, I tell you all what, I'll take my acre, along with Delle's acre, and Red will have to buy the house from the rest of us. At market value." OJ glares around the table, daring anyone to disagree with him.

Ellenor jumps up and slams her fist on the table. "OJ, shut your effing mouth." She stares at him, her eyes now a cold steel gray, daring him to say something.

The Snow men sit stone-faced around the table, and the dogs slink off the deck, tails between their legs. Ellenor sits back down shaking, but Red's gentle touch on her knee comforts her.

"Jesus Christ, you're all a pain in the ass. You always were."

They all look at their father the same as they did when they were kids—with trepidation and a bit of fear.

Ellenor places her clenched hands on the picnic table, her knuckles turning white from the grip. She feels perspiration trickling down her back. With a deep, silent inhale, she calmly addresses her father. "Dad, you've been a fine caretaker of this beautiful piece of land, and this is your decision. It's your land and your money. But if there is a way for you to stay here and keep it away from land predators, you would make Mom proud. She loved this place, and she taught each of us to cherish it as she did. Here is the name and contact information for that attorney. Do what you want with it. I've said my piece."

She gets up, walks around the table, and lightly touches her father's shoulder. "Let me know what you decide." As she turns to walk off the deck, she says, "Hey, one more thing, can someone please give those poor old dogs a bath?"

Ellenor gets on the bike, fighting back her tears, and peddles to her real home, the Callahan's.

Chapter Twenty-Three

"You are one decision away from a completely different life" – Mel Robbins

Esme

"Good morning" comes out as more of a command than a greeting. "Are they up?" Esme's face is flushed, and she's sweating and breathing through clenched teeth as she walks up the drive.

Mo stops walking across the yard and looks at Esme. As the youngest of the Callahan clan, she's used to all kinds of moods from her older sisters, including their friends.

Her hair, black like Emma's, hangs in a long braid down her back. Despite being in her early thirties, the freckles on her nose and the subtle lines framing her hazel eyes hint at early sun damage.

"No idea. You could always text them," she says sarcastically.

Esme ignores Mo's tone. Right now, she only cares about calming down and fixing this mess she has gotten herself into.

The cottage is empty, eerily quiet without Emma and Ellenor. She spots her cell phone next to the note she left them earlier this morning, which seems like a lifetime ago. Esme ignores the phone and hunts around for Ellenor's cigarettes. She peeks into the messy bedroom and sees the suitcases and clothes strewn about the floor. *The beach is a healthier choice than a cigarette.*

Her breathing has slowed down, along with her anger, but she is still humiliated. She returns to the kitchen and checks her phone for messages.

One from Emma.

> Gone to CBI. Come save me if I'm not
> back by 3.

One from Ellenor.

> Gone to talk to my dad about how to
> save his land. Send troops if I'm not back
> by noon.

And then she sees all the texts from Cody.

> Hey, I just wanted to be sure you made it
> safely to the Cape.

This annoys Esme. *Of course I made it safely. I could do the drive with my eyes closed.* She reads his next four texts.

> Hi, me again. Let me know you're okay.

> Hope your radio silence means you're
> having fun.

> ??????

Never mind

She puts her phone down and stares out the kitchen window, watching the movement of the waves. One thing you can depend on with waves, they always roll in and then roll back out. Her thoughts drift to Cody and what she said about him the other night. Nothing is wrong with him, they all agreed on that. He's a great guy, a wonderful father, and he loves her. Esme paces around the kitchen, unsettled, agitated, and unsure of what to do. She steps out to the front porch and sees Mo off to the right of the yard, weeding one of the flower beds.

Screw it. I know what I need right now. It's not Cody, and it's not Delle.

"Hey Mo, do you think your dad would let me borrow the Jeep for a while?" Her voice doesn't betray the uneasy dread that is lurking in her gut.

Mo looks up at Esme, wiping the dirt from her hands. "Why?"

"I want to go surfing, and I can't carry a board down those stairs. I'd kill myself. So I need to drive out to the beach."

Mo gets up from the garden bed and says matter-of-factly, "When was the last time you surfed?"

"I don't know—a while." Esme isn't hiding her look of angst and frustration very well, and Mo notices.

"Well, you probably would kill yourself carrying a long board down those stairs. And I'm not sure how good your chances are in the surf. Either way, stairs or waves, today might be your last day on earth," Mo says matter-of-factly, standing directly in front of Esme.

Esme's brown eyes are wide with surprise. She's floored by what Mo just said.

"Do you have a wet suit?" Mo asks.

"No."

"A rash guard?"

"No."

"A bathing suit?"

"Yes, of course."

Mo is starting to annoy her.

Mo wipes her hands on her jeans, studies Esme for a minute, and says, "Go get changed. I'll meet you out front."

"What?" Esme asks with a quizzical look. "What did you say?"

"Go change. I'll get the board and drive you to the beach. You know you won't make it down those stairs carrying a board, and you can't surf alone, you should know that. You haven't surfed since God knows when, which is even more reason for me to go." She tilts her head, her eyes narrowed, and says with a smirk, "Because from where I'm standing, you ain't got anyone but me."

Esme stares at Mo, wondering when Emma's bratty little sister became this forceful woman, giving her orders. *She might not look like Emma, but she sure sounds as bossy as Emma does sometimes.*

Mo parks the Jeep on the sand directly in front of her parent's property, gets out, and hands Esme a rash guard. "I parked here in case I need backup, although I don't think my parents can run down all those steps. And if you run into trouble, I'm not coming in to save you. The water is freezing."

Esme takes the rash guard and pulls it over her head. It's tight. "Thanks for your vote of confidence, Mo."

She carries the longboard to the water's edge and hesitates, surveying the water. The waves are relatively small. *Nothing I can't handle.* She puts on the leash and tugs it to make sure it's tight on her ankle. *Stop thinking, Esme. Just do it.* Esme steps in, gasping as the cold Atlantic Ocean hits her shins. She turns to see Mo standing, watching her. The look on her face propels Esme forward. She isn't going to let Maureen Callahan see her fail. She gets on the board, lies on her stomach, and begins paddling out to where the waves are breaking. The water is choppy, making it difficult to keep stable on the board and find her rhythm. Her arms and shoulders immediately begin to burn, but Esme continues, paddling through the waves coming at her. She instinctively pushes the nose of her board down into the water so she doesn't get smacked in the face. She makes it to the break and sits up on the board, panting, balancing with the motion of the sea. *What am I doing? Esme Agnes Prince, get a hold of yourself. Remember who you are, and where you come from. Remember how fearless you were. Remember, you know how to surf. Just freaking do this, girl.* With her board facing the shore, she watches over her left shoulder, looking for a wave she can handle. She decides to start slowly, letting a few sets pass her by while trying to settle in and get her bearings. She sees the telltale dark line out on the horizon—a set of waves is coming. Esme remembers the first one is usually the smallest, with larger waves coming in behind it. As the wave approaches, she lies on the board, steadies herself, and begins to paddle. She feels the force of the wave speeding up, pushing her board forward. With all her strength, Esme pops up and manages to ride the small wave close to shore without humiliating herself. Her passion and love of surfing, a feeling that she let fade away, comes roaring back, filling her with a fierce energy to keep going. Esme is exhilarated, her heart is racing, and she can't wait to catch another wave. This time, as she paddles out, her nerves are overtaken by an adrenaline rush that pushes her forward, to the break, to the waves. As soon as she's there, she sees another set coming her way. Esme waits, floating above the first wave, the salty air whipping her hair as she prepares for the next best wave. The second wave is more powerful, but she embraces the sense of her inherent surfing skills returning and rides the wave with renewed confidence to the edge of the shore. Without hesitation, Esme turns the board around, arms aching, and paddles back out to the waves. She does this over and over again, like a junkie who can't let the high go. The cold and the pain are the last things on her mind as she waits for the next set. She sees it, braces herself, and paddles over the first two. The third that's coming at her is slow to approach. Esme can see from where she's floating that this is going to be the biggest wave so far, and it's heading right for her. She's scared, but she remembers this fear. *My junkie adrenaline rush.* She prepares to catch this one or die trying. Esme steadies herself, takes a breath, lets it out, and begins paddling as fast as she can as the towering wall of water closes in on her. The force of this wave is powerful, pushing her board faster than the others did.

Esme grits her teeth and pops up on the board a moment before she would have wiped out and been pounded under the force of the wave. She stands, knees slightly bent, and cuts back on the wave to gain more power and keep this ride going as long as she can. She works with the wave as it brings her to the shore, saltwater stinging her eyes, the exhilarating feeling of freedom surging through her. Esme stumbles out of the water, out of breath, laughing out loud.

"Holy shit, you did it! I can't believe it." Mo is standing in the water next to her, laughing and clapping her hands.

Chapter Twenty-Four

"To move forward, you have to leave the past behind." — Susannah Cahalan

Emma

Emma tips the valet, gets in her car, and turns left to drive back to Orleans. Once CBI is out of her rearview mirror, she takes a breath. *What the hell is wrong with me? Why did I bolt out like that? Ben's a great guy—but is he? He could easily replace Ethan. But am I looking for someone to replace Ethan? Oh my God, I'm a mess.* She burst into tears. Sobbing, she pulls the car off to the side of the road, turns off the ignition, and leans her forehead onto the steering wheel, tears pouring down her face. She stays like this until there are no more tears, no more arguments in her head. *I don't need Ben to replace Ethan. I don't need anyone to replace him. I don't need anyone, period. Well, I do need myself.*

She lifts her head and realizes she has parked at Pleasant Bay Cove. This tranquil spot is surrounded by conservation land and shielded from the open ocean on three sides. The water is serene, perfect for swimming and sailing. The small, sandy beach is quiet today except for the sound of a woman's laugh as she tosses a tennis ball for her two dogs. Emma smiles. *Cape Cod black dogs.* Her family had a Cape Cod black dog when she was growing up—almost every family had at least one. She laughs at the memory of Esme complaining about her mother's refusal to let her have a dog. "I said no, Esme Agnes Prince, end of discussion." That's when Emma and Ellenor learned about Esme's middle name. They all understood that when Mrs. Prince used her middle name, she meant business.

The scene on the beach sets Emma in motion. Reaching for her camera bag in the backseat, she gets out of the car and approaches the woman and her dogs.

"Hi, are those your dogs?"

"Yup, they're mine, Johnny and June."

"Ah, you're a country music fan."

The woman smiles, nodding her head and tossing the ball again.

"Am I right to assume they're Cape Cod black dogs?"

"You are right. Johnny is the bigger one, black lab, of course, and who knows what he's mixed with. June"—she points to the dog carrying a stick—"she's a black lab, and we're pretty sure she's got some hound in her. But again, who knows? I'm impressed you know both country music and Cape Cod dogs." Despite the oversized black sunglasses and the Patriots ball cap concealing most of the woman's face, her smile is natural and inviting. "I'm Susan."

"Hi, I'm Emma. I grew up here, in Orleans." She tilts

her head to the left, the direction of home. "So I'm quite familiar with Cape Cod black dogs. I grew up with one, Rufus. And my older sister was—and probably still is—a big country music fan. She idolized Johnny Cash."

"Are you a photographer?" Susan asks, pointing to the camera bag.

Emma grins. "I am, and I was wondering if I could take some pictures of Johnny and June." She catches the look in Susan's eyes and fishes in her camera bag, pulling out a business card.

"Here, this proves I'm not a creepy stalker kind of person. Well, I hope it does," Emma says. Her violet eyes are sparkling, and her voice is energized. "I would love to snap some pictures of them, and I could send them to you. I photograph weddings and family events, baby showers, you name it, but it's always people, never pets." She leans in closer to Susan and says conspiringly, "I like animals more than people."

For the next half hour, Emma runs on the shore and chases the dogs into the water, snapping picture after picture. Susan throws the ball, and the three of them— Emma, Johnny, and June—race after it. She looks like a wild child, barefoot, black hair flying behind her. She's wet and sandy, and her laughter fills the salt air.

"I think I'm done," Emma says, trying to catch her breath.

Susan laughs as her dogs stand next to Emma, shaking off the water and sand. "I think they're done, too. Thank you for tiring them out."

"Thank you for letting me do this," Emma says, putting

her camera back in its bag. "This is more fun than I've had in a long time. I'll get these developed when I'm back in New York next week. I can't wait to hear what you think."

Emma walks off the beach, light as a feather, convinced this chance meeting was precisely the boost she needed.

"Mom? Dad? Anyone home?"

Her parents are sitting at the kitchen table going through their mail, drinking coffee.

"My goodness, Emma, you look like a drowned rat. What happened?" her mother asks.

Emma pulls a towel out of the closet and sets it on the chair to keep it dry. Her hair resembles shiny, tangled strands of black seaweed, and she knows she's a mess. Emma doesn't care.

"I've been running on the beach with some dogs. Sorry I'm a mess, but it is just what I needed. I need to talk to you guys about my business. When I was on the Vineyard, Grace told me that Dave has been promoted and they're moving to London."

Her father scowls. His eyes, similar to Emma's, cloud over. "Where does that leave you and the business?"

"Good question, and that's why I'm here. Dave emailed a few options I want to go over with you. Before I start, though, I've made one decision already. I let Dave know about it once I had digested Grace's bombshell and could look at his proposals with a clear head."

Her mother scrapes her chair on the old tile floor, moving in closer to the table and focusing her eyes on Emma. "What decision is that, dear?"

"I'm not going to buy them out. I don't want to run the business without Grace. We are—we were—a great team, and I know I don't want to start all over again trying to keep the business going. After I made that clear to them, Dave came up with these options."

"That sounds reasonable. Let's hear what Dave had to say."

Despite her wet hair and disheveled clothes, Emma's mother seems to notice her confident gaze and bright eyes.

"The first option is Grace stays for the summer, and we finish it out together. People hired us, E&G Photography, for a reason, and we need to honor our commitments to those booked gigs. During the summer, we hire another photographer. I give it a full twelve months to decide if I want to buy out Grace."

Her father looks skeptical. "But you said you don't want to do that."

His wife places her hand on his. "Go on then. What's option two?"

"Right, I know that. But Dave is keeping all the options on the table for now. Option two is similar to the first one. Dave leaves, Grace stays until Labor Day, but we sell the business outright as soon as possible. I would stay on until the first of the year to help the new owners set up for success. And before you say anything, there is an option three. We close up shop in September, which neither of us wants to do. That would mean we'd leave our fall clients in the lurch. We'd have to send out a press release soon so people could look somewhere else for their events."

"Is there a market to sell your business?" Her mother's eyes dart between her daughter and her husband, a worried crease forming on her forehead.

"According to Dave, there is." She puts her hands flat on the table and says, "I don't know what to do, and I don't have a lot of time to decide."

"How are you set financially? Even if you get something from the sale of the business, where does that leave you? I don't want to see you struggling at this stage of your life."

Emma gets up to pour herself a glass of water and gazes out the kitchen window at the ocean. She can see someone surfing, which is unusual for that section of the beach. But it makes her smile.

"Dad, you don't need to worry about me at this stage of my life," she says teasingly.

She sits back down at the table and looks at her parents. The years have etched themselves into their faces. *They're getting older. We all are getting older.*

"Dave has been a financial godsend to me. He has been handling my investments and, as of today, I don't need to work another day in my life if I don't want to." She omits that Dave also saved her financially when she was at her lowest point. Dave kept her afloat, handling her money and paying her bills when Ethan left her. But Emma doesn't share that with her parents. They're oblivious to how close she came to never climbing out of the black hole from Ethan's betrayal. She wants to keep it that way.

"Mom, where are you going?" Emma asks when her mother gets out of her chair and walks toward the living room.

"I'm getting some paper. We are going to start a list of each option, with the pros and cons. And we are also going to figure out what you want, Emma. We are going to come up with option four."

Chapter Twenty-Five

"Nothing soothes the soul like a walk on a
Cape Code beach." – Unknown

Ellenor

"Hello?"

"Hi, Maggie."

"Ellenor, this is a surprise. A nice one."

Ellenor's face brightens as she pictures Maggie's smile, an image as vivid as if she were sitting next to her, not on the other side of the country.

"I'm good. It's hard to believe, but being at home has actually been enjoyable. I've had time to think, rejuvenate my soul, and breathe in the Cape Cod salt air. This has been a surprisingly good visit for the most part. At least nobody died," she says with a laugh.

"That sounds like exactly what you needed. I'm glad you've had this time. Anything else?" Maggie asks with a hint of hope in her question.

"Yes," she answers hesitantly. "I've thought a lot about our time in Nantucket."

Silence.

Ellenor is nervous. *Am I making a big mistake?*

"Maggie, I'm confused. I know we decided to take this slow, but no matter how many beach walks I've done, I can't figure this out."

"What can't you figure out, Ellenor?" Maggie's voice is warm and soothing.

"I can't figure out us. I care for you, but I just don't know what to do. I've never done this before."

"Done what, Ellenor? Had feelings for another person? Are you confused because we are two women who might want to explore a sincere relationship?"

"Yes. I think so."

"Let me ask you a question. Think back to when you were younger. Did you ever have feelings for a girl in your class or your neighborhood? Something that was different from what you have for Emma and Esme?"

"I didn't grow up in a neighborhood. I grew up at the end of a dirt road." Ellenor is annoyed with this question. She absentmindedly digs a hole in the sand with a clam shell, mesmerized as she watches the grains slide back in, filling the hole.

Maggie is probably thinking, *Same old Ellenor.*

"Okay, did you look at a girl and think she's pretty? I like her smile. Things like that? What did you think about girls when you were growing up? How about boys? What about when you moved into adolescence? Were you confused then?"

"I didn't think about anything. I was too busy playing on the beach, surfing, and sailing. I was busy all the time, fishing and clamming in the summer. In the fall, I'd spend hours hiking in the woods or riding horses on the beach. We cross-country skied and skated on the cranberry bogs in the winter. My days were filled with school, household chores, and then part-time jobs when I was older. There was no room in my mind to consider anything beyond the challenges of surviving high school and my family."

"That's why you are such a gifted author," Maggie says with a sense of pride in her tone.

"Huh?"

"You've suppressed most of your emotions since you were a kid. They've been there— they've always been there —simmering below the surface, patiently waiting for you to acknowledge them. Your writing is an extension of yourself —your experiences and memories, good or bad. Your words are who you are, Ellenor Snow, and that's why I love you."

Ellenor moves the phone from her ear and stares out at the ocean, tears in her eyes.

"Ellenor? Are you still there?"

"I am, sorry. I don't know what to say. You've rendered me speechless."

Maggie laughs. "Well, that's a first. Listen, please. No matter what you decide about us, whether there is even a possibility of us taking this somewhere, I will always be your friend and, hopefully, your agent. I'm here for you. Believe it or not, I struggled for years before I was honest with myself. But I had a sense of being different from what was expected of me since I was a kid. Knowing it, embracing it, and believing in myself helped me face the hurdles society tried to place in front of me. And what do you think I did? I barged right through those effing hurdles, leaving them in my dust… Ellenor, everyone has a journey of some kind—none of them are the same."

Ellenor takes a deep, cleansing breath, filling her lungs with salt air. "I have an idea for the next book."

Maggie may wish for a different response, but the agent in her replies, "That's very positive news—care to fill me in?"

"It's percolating in my brain right now, but I'm excited about writing again. I think I'll name it *When We Were Mermaids.*"

"Interesting. I can't wait to hear more."

"Just one other thing. I'm coming home. I'm coming home to you, Maggie."

Ellenor remains sitting in the sand as she thinks about everything Maggie just said to her. *Maybe I am good at what I do. Maybe Maggie is right.* She takes a minute to process the conversation, looking down the beach and watching a surfer gracefully catch a wave. *That's not Esme, is it?*

Chapter Twenty-Six

"A friend is someone who knows all about
you and loves you just the same."
— Elbert Hubbard

Revelations

Esme is riding high on endorphins, a feeling she hasn't
experienced in years, her heart pounding with exhilaration.

Mo is at the edge of the shore, laughing and jumping
up and down as she hands Esme a large beach towel.

"Damn, girl, you were amazing out there. I am blown
away by you. You are beaming!" Mo says, her smile and
hazel eyes wide with admiration.

Esme wraps herself in the beach towel, shakes the water
dripping from her wet curls, and laughs. "I think it's
because my face is frozen from the cold water. I can't stop
smiling. Mo, thank you for doing this for me. You have no
idea how much I appreciate it."

"Esme, the look on your face is all I need for thanks.
Damn, Esme, you have restored my faith in aging," she says
with a smile.

Out of the corner of her eye, Esme notices someone running down the beach toward them, frantically waving their arms. "Is that Ellenor running down the beach like a lunatic?" Then she hears someone yelling her name. "Is that Emma, running down the stairs, also looking like a crazy person?"

"Yup, that's my sister, and I think that's Ellenor coming toward us."

Ellenor and Emma run up to them, winded, laughing, their words tumbling over each other.

"Holy shit, Esme, I can't believe you," says Emma.

"Are you out of your mind? Don't answer. You are fearless," adds Ellenor.

Esme laughs. "I don't know about fearless, but crazy—yes."

"I'm leaving the Jeep for you guys. I can walk home. Oh, and I left a little something for you in the way back." Mo walks away, grinning from ear to ear.

"What in the world were you thinking, Esme?" Emma asks. "You could have drowned or gotten knocked on the head by the board—and then drowned."

"I've had a day that went from a terrible decision to the worst outcome imaginable. When I got back to the cottage, I thought I'd explode, and I didn't care if I did. I figured if I was going to blow into a million little pieces, I might as well go out doing something I love."

"Esme"—Ellenor leans in closer—"we've said this forever, and as long as we breathe, we will keep saying that we will always have each other's backs. What the hell happened today?"

Esme stares out at the ocean, silent for a moment, watching the waves come crashing to shore. *Do I dare? If Ellenor was strong enough to tell us she's falling for Maggie, I can do this.*

She shivers, wrapped in the wet towel. "I need to get out of this wet suit."

While Esme changes in the back seat of the Jeep, Emma lays out the large beach blanket Mo left for them and gets three beers from the cooler.

"I woke up in a mood." Taking the beer from Emma, Esme still feels exhilarated by what she just accomplished. "I was unsettled, anxious, whatever you want to call it. But I knew the reason, and I knew today was the day I had to figure it out, no excuses. Do I move on, or do I move ahead and embrace the life I have?"

"What does that even mean? Is this about Cody?"

"No, Emma, this is about me." Inhaling deeply to calm herself, Esme says, "I went to see Delle."

"Oh, that's why he was so quiet at my dad's. Oh, sorry, I didn't mean to interrupt." Ellenor takes a sip of the cold beer, waiting for what Esme will say next.

"He was quiet at your dad's?" Esme shakes her head to clear any lingering thoughts of Delle from her mind. "Anyway, I decided to go and see Delle at his house. Aren't either of you curious why I went to see him this morning?"

"No" is the response.

"What, why? Seriously, don't you want to know why I went over there?"

Emma moves to face Esme on the blanket, sitting on her knees. "We have a pretty good idea, and it wasn't to check on the updates he's made to the house. We haven't talked about this in a long time—I hope you found what you're looking for. Either way, whatever happened, it's your business. No judgment."

"You haven't talked about what for a long time?" she responds, clearly irritated.

"Esme, we've always suspected something was going on between you and Delle in high school. We just never wanted to say anything." Ellenor finishes her beer, wishing she had savored it for what seemed to be a ripping-off-the-bandage conversation for Esme.

Esme is flabbergasted. Not only because of what she thought was a secret between her and Delle, but because her friends never let on they knew—never even let on what they thought they knew.

"I'm shocked. I don't know what to say. What exactly do you think you know?"

"Don't get all defensive. Ellenor and I are on your side. The truth is, you've always been private about your relationships with guys. That's who you are, and we respect that. But what has me a little bit worried is what happened today. What sent you charging into the ocean?"

"Is there anything stronger than beer in the cooler?" Esme asks.

Emma walks to the back of the jeep and opens the hatch door to find a picnic basket packed to the brim. "Finally, that little sister of mine has learned a thing or two from me. Tequila, anyone?"

Esme zips up her gray sweatshirt, hood over her wet curls, sips the tequila, and begins. "I had a crush on Delle since I was in middle school. Honestly, I know it sounds ridiculous, but he said he felt the same way. We started flirting in junior high, and one thing led to another. It wasn't any big deal, and to be honest, I thought we did a great job of hiding it—apparently not."

"If you liked each other, why hide it? Were you ashamed to be seen with a Snow boy?" Ellenor's voice is sharp, her words a mixture of insecurity and sarcasm.

"Ellenor, absolutely not," Esme responds defensively. "For one thing, he's your brother, and you hate your brothers. I was afraid to tell you. And my mother would never have allowed me to date Delle. Not because he's a Snow, but because she hates all men. She never wanted me to date anyone."

"Go on," says Ellenor, not sounding convinced.

"Things pretty much ended for us when Delle graduated high school and joined the Coast Guard. It's not like we talked about what we'd do while we were apart from each other. He didn't ask me to wait for him and I didn't ask him to do the same. We didn't write, we didn't talk, we seemed to be done."

"Did you want to be done?"

"I don't know. I was caught up in my own little world back then. Chalk it up to being a shallow teenager with a mother who was relentless about my weight, my clothes, and what was I going to do with my life. I'm sure I didn't give Delle much thought then. My escape was surfing. That's all I cared about. Then Cody and I started dating. Delle was in my rearview mirror. Or so I thought."

Ellenor takes her last sip of tequila, listening to Esme as

she walks over to the Jeep for a refill. With her back to Esme, she asks, "Did you and Delle get together when he came home for spring break, our senior year?"

"Yes" is the hushed reply. "But that's when Delle and I made a pact to stay away from each other."

Esme is quiet, Emma is quiet, and Ellenor looks at them both with trepidation.

Dear God, how do I say this? But she doesn't hold back.

Ellenor asks the question she has been harboring for years. "Is CJ Delle's son?"

Esme jumps up from the beach blanket and steadies herself on the uneven sand. "Absolutely not. Cody is his father." Her voice, high pitched and trembling, rises in indignation. "How can you ask me that?"

"Hey, let's all calm down. Both of you come sit back down. I'm going to put out the food Mo brought. I think we all need some sustenance. It's been a rough day for all of us."

"Are you trying to steer this conversation away from the fact that CJ could be my nephew?" Ellenor says forcefully. Her voice is strained with the fear of her words.

"Ellenor Snow, stop right this minute, or I'm going to punch you in the throat," Emma says. "We both know that Cody's his father, not Delle. The facts are that Esme and Delle had something going on years ago, and when Delle left, it ended. Or partially ended."

Emma glances at Esme, whose jaw is clenched so tightly

her teeth are almost grinding, and her narrowed eyes betray her anger.

"Esme, it's okay. I said before, no judgment. Ellenor and I have plenty of messy stuff that we've tried to keep to ourselves. Esme, please sit down."

Ellenor glares at her.

"Well, at least I have plenty of stuff," Emma says, trying to smooth things over.

"Ellenor, I can't believe you would ask me that question. Did this just pop into your head, or have you been stewing on it for years?"

"It just popped into my head," Ellenor lies, unable to return Esme's stare. "I'm sorry, but, well… I'm sorry." Ellenor's words taste bitter, and why not? They have been stewing for years.

Regaining her composure, Esme sits up as straight as she can on the blanket and begins again. "For the sake of our friendship, I am going to forgive your stupid question. I'm sure your inquiring minds aren't done with me, so I will bare my soul to you as we've done with each other since the dawn of time. I'm done with Delle, and today proved to me he would never be the man that Cody is. Cody loves me and will probably do anything for me. And I love him, love my life with CJ and him. I thought I could recapture who I used to be, and foolishly, I thought I could do that by being with Delle. I'm not sure why I think, or thought, I need a guy for that. What I needed was to find myself, and I did— on that last exhilarating, terrifying wave. Now, can we please move on?"

"Cheers to that. Who needs men, anyway?" Ellenor

says, raising her red cup before mouthing "I'm sorry" to Esme.

Esme smiles at Ellenor, finishes her tequila before the others, and lies on the blanket, eyes closed. *Why won't this day end?*

"Speaking of men, I hung out with Ben today." Emma sees the look of confusion on Ellenor's face. "Ben, the handsome running guy on the beach, remember?"

"Ah, how could I forget—he is quite unforgettable. Tell us everything." Ellenor sneaks a look at Esme then snickers and says, "Well, as much as you want."

"Oh, you know, just a typical day slumming around the pool at CBI, drinking champagne."

Esme sits up, intrigued by any conversation that doesn't involve her, Cody, or Delle, and better yet, one that involves a handsome man. "Emma, we could use a few more details, since Ellenor and I don't typically lounge around the CBI pool."

Emma sits cross-legged, filling her friends in on her day with Ben. She tells them everything—how she initiated it all with one early morning phone call, what she wore, the fabulous lobster rolls, and what champagne they drank.

"And now, for the important stuff. God, he is so easy to look at and to talk to. He seems like an open book. He talked about his disaster of an engagement to a woman named Michelle. At least, I think that's her name. He seems to like his family, who sound supportive but maybe a bit smothering. We have a lot in common."

"But? Hold on, I'm getting a refill." Esme doesn't want to miss any little detail. But standing behind the Jeep, she slowly refills the cups, her hands trembling slightly as she tries to pull herself together in the wake of Ellenor's outburst. *I can do this. I can do this. If I can remember how to surf, I can do anything.*

"Yes, there's a 'but,'" Emma says as Esme returns. "I'm still reeling from Ethan's less-than-enlightening talk the other night, so I might not be in the right frame of mind to think about starting something with Ben or anyone. Plus, there is something there, you guys. I don't know, but there seems to be some kind of undercurrent with him. Just not sure if my intuition works anymore." She sees the expression on Esme and Ellenor's faces, and it's clear she can't end the conversation here. "Red flags—I sense red flags." She raises her hand, silencing Esme before she can interrupt. "There's nothing specific, just a feeling—sometimes the tone of his voice made me… concerned, if that's even the right word."

Esme nods her head in agreement. "Okay, good for you for picking up on that. How did you leave it with him?"

"I pretty much bolted. I pretended I needed to get home, said goodbye, and walked away. It was a shitty thing for me to do. I need to apologize, and I will. But I have even bigger news that doesn't involve a man."

"Esme, pass me the chips and guacamole," Ellenor says. "I think I need more food for whatever's coming next."

"Grace and I are selling the business," Emma continues. "I've been keeping this to myself until I knew what I wanted to do. And I want to sell it. It goes on the market at the end of the month, although Dave's pretty confident that he already has an interested buyer lined up.

Ellenor jumps up from the blanket, spilling chips, and Esme yells, "Shut up! What? Why?"

"No interruptions, you guys. The plan is that E&G will shut down at the end of the year. We'll honor the gigs we have scheduled, but that's it. Grace and Dave are moving to London, which is what triggered this chain of events. Dave's leaving in a few weeks, and Grace will stay through the summer. I'll help the new owners with the transition up until January. I am a free woman in six months. Let's toast to that, mermaids!"

"Good God," Ellenor says, "I don't know if I can compete with the day you two have had or if I even want to." She's quiet for a moment, a frown creasing her forehead as she turns a smooth beach stone in her hand.

"I went to my dad's this morning, armed with all the information your dad gave me, in an attempt to help him save the property. I had told my brothers to be there but didn't say why. Well, one of those jerks must have told OJ, because he was there."

"Oh, not good." Esme's upper lip curls in a snarl.

"It's never good when OJ is around, and today was no exception. God, even the sight of him makes me want to smash him over the head with a hammer. Anyway, the conversation went about as well as you might expect. Not well. Red tried to back me up. And like I said, Delle was quiet, although he did say he didn't want any part of the property."

Esme's eyes are fixed on Ellenor. She listens closely, her face a mask revealing nothing when Delle's name is mentioned.

"So, what's the decision? Is there one?"

"Good question, Emma. There is no decision. Shocking, I know." Ellenor says it sarcastically, but her voice catches. "My father wants to give each of us an acre. Delle doesn't want his acre, Red just wants to stay at the house with Dad, and OJ wants everyone's acres. They are all such a bunch of stubborn idiots." Ellenor puts her hands on her face and shakes her head, tears forming in the corners of her eyes.

"What do *you* want, Ellenor?" Emma's voice is soft and nurturing.

Ellenor knows this voice—it's the voice of Mrs. Callahan. It's the voice of her two best friends, and surprisingly, to her, it's the voice of Maggie.

She raises her head, fighting back the tears, and stares out at the ocean. "How can I turn my back on this place again? How can I leave you two? I'm so conflicted. I want to save my dad's place. My soul is there, but I can't be there. I'm torn about so much, you guys."

Emma jumps up to hug Ellenor. Instead, she trips on the blanket and falls on top of her, sending chips, guacamole, and solo cups in different directions. Emma can't stop laughing, and she can't get off of Ellenor, who is crying, laughing, and yelling for her to get off. With a playful leap, Esme jumps on top of them, prompting screams of "Get off! Get off!" and clumsy attempts to stand, each one stumbling back down and laughing with abandon. It takes a few minutes before they can get off of each other, still laughing, shake the sand out of their hair, and toss the spilled chips for the seagulls.

"Okay, that was a great way to end a conversation," Esme says. "But honestly, Ellenor, what are you going to do?"

"I'm going to have my attorney draft some kind of legal document, carefully worded to avoid sending my father further off the deep end than he already is, stating I accept his gift of one acre and am offering to buy five more at market value."

"And?"

"You can never just leave things alone, can you, Esme? The 'and' is I'm going to go to my second home, San Francisco, and I'm going to grow my hair long." Ellenor beams and continues, "I'm going to write my next book, *When We Were Mermaids*, and—are you ready? I am going to give myself permission to fall in love with Maggie O'Hare. Let's toast to that!"

As the sun dips into the ocean, the moon rises, casting a silvery light and bathing the water in a magical glow.

Silently, Emma rises and walks to the edge of the water, Esme and Ellenor follow. The ocean is now as smooth as glass, its waves lapping at the shore, the gulls gliding overhead without a sound, leaving the beach in an eerie stillness. They lock eyes, strip down to their underwear, and walk hand in hand into the ocean.

Chapter Twenty-Seven

"A friend is someone who gives you total
freedom to be yourself." — Jim Morrison

Emma

S quinting against the bright June sun, Emma waves
goodbye, following Esme's sporty red Audi on foot
until it disappears around the bend of the shell driveway,
her friend's surf tunes blaring and caramel curls blowing in
the breeze.

She turns to look across her parents' property and the
ocean beyond.

"It's been one hell of a week," she says out loud and
smiles. *One hell of a week, for sure.*

Her thoughts are interrupted by a text.

> I ran into your sister in town, she said the
> E's have left. Want some company?

*Damn you, Mo, for telling Delle that Esme and Ellenor are
gone. Damn you, Delle, just in principle.*

Sure, come on over. I don't have any plans.

Send.

Soon, the familiar sound of Delle's black Ford pickup announces his arrival outside Callahan's Cottage. Emma is sitting on the porch steps. Her black hair is tucked behind her ears, and her long, tan legs begin where her short cut-off jeans end.

"You're looking delicious this morning, Emma Callahan." His blue-gray eyes twinkle as he hands her a cup of coffee. "I thought you could use this since the E's are gone, meaning your resident chef is gone."

"You know we hate being called that, but thank you—thank you for the coffee. Which, by the way, I am quite capable of making myself." She takes a sip, and it is much better than what she could have brewed up.

"Since when?" Delle laughs, following her up the stairs. They sit together on the wicker couch, sipping their coffees, the warmth of the sun on their faces. Emma lets out a soft sigh, basking in the simple comfort of Delle, her long-time friend, and the silent words passing between them.

"So, aside from the night at the Pequod, how's your trip back home been?"

Emma gives Delle a sideward glance and shakes her head. "It was great, except for that night, as I'm sure you know. I don't think I thanked you for bringing back our bikes and feeding us the next day."

"No thanks needed. I hope you know by now that I'm always here for you."

Emma melts, just a bit. Delle has been there for her as long as she can remember.

"So, tell me all about your week with those two. Seeing the three of you together sure brought back some memories. My damn sister hasn't changed a bit. Still as bullheaded as always. You should have heard her talking to my dad about the property. I swear she's the only one who can stand up to him. Except for my mother, of course. She always stood up to old Ordelle—wouldn't take any of his crap."

"I think tenacious is a more accurate description of Ellenor. I hope her attempt to talk some sense into your dad worked."

"Only time will tell." He's quiet for a minute, sipping his coffee, as if carefully planning his next words. "It was good to see Esme. When was the last time you both saw each other?"

Emma bristles when she hears Esme's name coming from Delle. "You know how long it's been. Why would you ask that? I heard she was over at your place. Did she interrupt something between you and Mary Pembroke?" Emma is annoyed at how whiny she sounds.

Delle leans in close, saying, "You know I don't kiss and tell."

She laughs. "One of your better qualities. Hey, let's go for a swim. The tide is perfect, unless, of course, you don't have a suit," she says suggestively.

"Suit's in the truck. I'll meet you on the beach."

The morning is cool, and the water is cooler, but that doesn't stop these two Cape Cod townies from racing each other into the small waves. Townies or not, they both give a shout as they hit the water, the cold sending shock waves through their bodies. Without hesitation, Delle dives in, with Emma right behind him. They surface, push their hair out of their eyes, and catch their breath as they tread water. Delle dives back down and grabs Emma by the ankles. She screams and kicks him away, trying to push him back down when he surfaces. She dives under a small wave, and Delle swims out farther to the larger waves. When Emma comes up for air, she panics for a split second. *Where's Delle?* Then she spots him. She smiles, relieved to see him catching a decent-sized wave, body-surfing toward her. This moment echoes memories from their childhood, something they took for granted—the gift of swimming, surfing, and playing in the ocean in their backyard. Delle pops up from the foam of the wave and swims over to Emma. He moves close and says, "Your lips are blue." He pulls her close to kiss her gently. "Let's get out and dry off."

They sit side by side on a beach blanket, wrapped in towels, and look out to the ocean without speaking. The two share a sense of familiarity, something they both know intimately. Delle is on his back, propped up on his elbows, and Emma is sitting cross-legged as she sifts sand between her hands.

"This is nice. Just like old times," Delle says, breaking the silence. He gently traces his fingers along her tanned forearm and continues, "I don't want to spoil the mood, but you told me you had some decisions to make, and I'm wondering if you've made them. You don't need to tell me, of course, but you got me curious."

She wipes the sand off her hands and looks at Delle. *God, I would love to just crawl into his arms right now.*

"I think I've figured some things out. At least I hope I have." She shrugs her shoulders, her smile uncertain.

Emma turns to face Delle, her eyes fixed on him as she fills him in on her recent life-changing events and the choices she has made. She doesn't hold back telling him about Grace and Dave moving to London and how that shook her faith in her self-worth. Here is another person she loves walking out of her life, with no thought of what it will do to her. Delle sits up, listening attentively, not saying a word. Emma explains Dave's proposals and how they finally agreed to put the business on the market immediately. Grace will stay on to help with the transition for the summer, then leave in September. Emma will stay until the end of the year.

"So, what do you think?" she asks, looking for a reaction.

"That's a lot to take in. When does the business go up for sale? How do you feel about that? You and Grace have established a good name for yourselves—won't that be hard to walk away from?"

"I am damn proud of what we created, and I've thrived on the energy we put into our work. That's what motivated me, kept me going, and spurred me to improve my craft. But to be completely honest, I haven't been feeling that for a while now—specifically at the wedding shoots. It's hard for me to admit, but more often than not, I find I can't relate to the happy newlyweds. That distance I place between us makes it difficult to capture what is supposed to be one of the happiest days in a person's life. I'm not sure if I'm burned out, or what it is. But I need a big change, a clean slate, a fresh start, whatever you want to call it. As soon as I gave my go-ahead, Dave put E&G on the market, and we already have a few interested buyers. The sooner this becomes a done deal, the sooner I can reinvent myself." Emma stops talking, shakes her head, and looks out to the ocean again. In a quiet voice, she says, "I don't know why I'm not over what Ethan did. But one thing I've learned in therapy is that grief has no timeline. It's a long uphill climb to find peace, but I'm not giving up."

"Trust the process. You'll get there when you're supposed to get there. You've made great strides over the last few years—be proud of that. I'm curious to know what the new Emma Callahan will look like. I hope she doesn't change too much. I like her just the way she is," Delle says in a soft tone.

Emma reaches for her phone in the beach bag and moves closer to Delle. She takes a few minutes scrolling.

"Emma?"

She raised her hand. "Hold on, here it is. Check these out."

"What am I looking at?"

"Just swipe to the right—you'll see."

He does as she says and scrolls through pictures of dogs on the beach. Puzzled, Delle hands her phone back. "Okay, pictures of Cape Cod black dogs. What do they have to do with anything?"

Emma hands the phone back to him. "Look closer, I know it's hard to see on the phone, but try. Do you see anything beyond two dogs romping on the beach? Does anything stand out besides the obvious?" She's nervous. *This must be how Ellenor feels when she shows someone her first draft of a new book. What if I've made a huge mistake, and I suck at taking pictures of anything not human?*

"Well, besides the obvious, the dogs, the sand, and the water, I get a sense of the scene. It's less about what I see, and more about the vibe. Some of these shots seem to bring out the playfulness in these two mutts, not a freaking care in the world. I'm not kidding when I say these shots come through with a sensation of being completely unburdened —just absolute downright joy. You took these?" He looks at her, his face a mixture of pride and amazement.

Emma's beaming smile illuminates her face. She springs from the beach blanket and dances in the sand, not caring who sees her or what she looks like. "I did. I took those pictures, and you felt what I was feeling when I took them. Holy shit, I can do this."

Delle stays seated, admiring, grinning, and adoring Emma. He's known her all her life, from the bratty little troublemaker friend of his sister to the emerging beauty in middle school, and then she became Ethan's girl. She was always Ethan's girl.

Emma collapses on the blanket, laughing and winded. She takes her phone from him, tucks it in the beach bag, and says, "Thank you, Delle. Thank you for getting me, for always believing in me, and for always being here for me."

He takes her hand again, locks eyes, and says in a soft, sincere tone, "I'm always going to be here for you, which begs the question—what's next? Where will you be, and just exactly what will you be doing?" He pauses before saying, "Is there a little space in your next life for me?"

"Of course there will be space for you. My goodness, that's a silly question. I don't know what I would have done without you for these last five years. Ellenor and Esme are my anchors, but they can't give me what you can."

"Great sex?" he asks, grinning provocatively.

"No. And shut up—I'm serious," she says, swatting his arm. Emma gazes at the ocean, always finding solace in its vastness. "I should have come here right after Ethan left. I'm not sure why I didn't. We all know the ocean cures everything."

"You can't go back in time, Emma. Tell me, what is it you plan to do with your one wild and precious life?"

Emma stares at Delle in amazement. "Did you just quote Mary Oliver?" She gives him an incredulous look.

"Guilty. It's probably the only thing I remember from high school English," he says sheepishly.

"I'm impressed you remember that poem, "The Summer Day." It's one of my favorites. She was a gifted writer, and that she lived on the Cape makes her even more special. And to answer your question, I'm heading back to the city tomorrow. I dread it, but I need to switch my flip-flops for street shoes and get acclimated to the real world again before our next photo shoot. My plan is to start a new business, and your reaction to my pictures of the 'two mutts,' as you called them, sealed the deal. I'm going to focus on photographing animals, mostly dogs, to start. People love their pets, especially the ones in the city. I want to take those pampered pets out of their comfort zones and capture their joy and excitement off a leash. Well, at least that's the plan. What about you? Do you have anything in the works? Ya know, marriage, kids," she says teasingly."

"Your next adventure sounds like a solid move for you. No people, only animals. Sounds ideal to me. But no, I don't have any grand announcements or plans. I'm spending the summer fishing and building up my charter business."

He hesitates, turning a shell round and round in his hand. "You know, I guess I do have a plan, or a dream. I want to have the most successful charter business on the Cape, maybe on the coast of New England. My mother used to say go for the gold, so why not? And you know I don't have any plans for kids, or marriage. That ship sailed a long time ago. Let's go back up, I need to get out of this wet suit and move on with my day."

Delle stands, offering Emma his hand to help her from the blanket. His body language makes it clear he's done talking. She takes his hand, feeling the strength in his grip as he pulls her up. She leans into Delle, giving him a warm, tight hug. The scent of the ocean lingering in his hair fills her senses. They walk up the steep stairs to Callahan's Cottage, Delle carrying the beach blanket and towels, Emma carrying the beach bag. They stop at the top and admit they're out of breath, then they laugh at how age and life are trying to sneak up on them.

Delle hands Emma the towels and stands looking out to the ocean instead of at her. His shoulders are straight, his chin is jutted out, and he says with some resignation, "So I guess this is goodbye."

Emma steps closer to Delle, their fingers brushing

lightly as they both gaze at the endless expanse of the ocean before them.

"We'll never say goodbye, Delle. I think I might be back here in January to give Mo a break from my parents. You know we'll stay in touch. We always will."

Emma takes a breath and says with softness and conviction, "Don't give up. Your ship might have sailed"—she shrugs her shoulders—"and now it's looking for a safe harbor. Either let her go completely or do something. Remember, 'It is better for the heart to break, than not to break.'"

"Mary Oliver?"

"Yup. See you soon. Be well, Delle."

She watches the black Ford pickup drive away, hoping it isn't the last time she sees this truck at Callahan's Cottage but feeling maybe this is what is meant to be.

Chapter Twenty-Eight

"Friendship has splendors that love
knows not." — Mariama Bâ

Esme

Esme watches Emma in the rearview mirror as her friend follows her down the driveway, waving and looking casually stunning and sexy at the same time in her cut-off jean shorts and white V-neck T-shirt. *Emma has always been the beautiful one.* She puts the Audi into overdrive and steps on the gas. She's feeling a bit deflated this morning after yesterday's lows and highs, first Delle and then the waves. *Focus on the waves. Focus on the waves.*

Last night was bittersweet—not how she expected her last night at Callahan's Cottage to go. She's miffed that her high of surfing was overshadowed by the turn of events. Somehow, she went from 'holy shit, look what I did' to Ellenor asking her if CJ was Delle's son.

Esme slows the car, realizing she's going sixty in a thirty-mile-an-hour zone. Esme Prince or not, the cops won't let her get away with that. She drives through town, past the

Old Pequod Inn onto Main Street, and pulls over. *I just need to breathe. Last night—our last night together—and I'm leaving more stressed than when I arrived.*

An older woman walking her dog glares at Esme as she walks by. Esme shakes her head of crazy curls, turns the music down then completely off. *What the fuck? What the ever-loving fuck.*

She sits in the car, replaying last night in her head.

Screw Ellenor. How dare she ask that about CJ? I should've gotten up and left. But oh no, Esme would never do that. I held it together, did my best to let go of what she said, chalk it up to Ellenor being Ellenor. Once I did that, we all got back to our usual selves. Or at least pretended to. But later that night, things went downhill. All I did was say I was opting out of getting up early the next morning to say goodbye to Ellenor. She had to leave at five thirty in the morning, and I said I would love to sleep in just one morning before I got back to work. Ellenor's feelings got hurt, or something like that, and she got mad. She said I wake up at that ungodly hour every day, but I couldn't bother to get up to say goodbye to her.

I think I smoothed things over when I said, 'I'm saying my goodbyes tonight. I hate goodbyes. They are the end of something wonderful. I hate beginnings because you don't know how they're going to turn out. I guess I like the middle of things. Like a good éclair. I can skip the top and the bottom crust—just give me the filling.'

I love these women, but damn, sometimes I wish we weren't so intense.

Esme readjusts her seat belt, pulls down the rearview visor, and checks her reflection. She's not looking for wrin-

kles or food in her teeth. Esme is looking for herself, yet
again. She looks at her phone. "Siri, tell Cody I'm leaving
the Cape. I'll be home soon." She turns the music up loud,
singing along with the Go Go's. "Vacation, all I ever
wanted. Vacation, have to get away."

As she merges onto Route 6, she attempts to adjust her
attitude and drive within the speed limit and the flow of the
traffic.

"Siri, call Roseanne."

"Hi, Esme."

"Hey, Roseanne, I'm happy to hear your voice. You've
survived without me."

"We have, but we've missed you. OMG, you can't
believe how the Armstrongs, you know, the parents from
the CBI wedding, went on and on about how blown away
—my words, not theirs—they were about the wedding.
They wanted to thank you in person. I think I said you were
barfing behind the porta potties."

"Roseanne, you did not."

She laughs. "Leave me again at one of these fancy gigs
and you'll see."

"Well, that's what I want to talk to you about. How
would you feel if you did all the fancy gigs?"

"That's just mean, Esme."

"Not if you like what I have baking in my brain,
Roseanne. I'm crossing the Sagamore Bridge now and
should be in town in about an hour, depending on the traffic. Can we talk then?"

"Sure, but should I be worried?"

"I hope you'll be excited, not worried. But let's talk. Oh, no matter what, you have a job."

Esme changes the music to Fleetwood Mac and steps on the gas. "Silver Springs" comes on, and she thinks back to that mind-boggling night at the Pequod, all of them together again—just like old times, but not really. *Those days are over.* She turns her focus to the road as she passes the exits to Plymouth, then Duxbury and Hingham. Esme's getting close to Boston, home, and Cody.

She pulls into her parking spot in the garage, puts the top up, and gets her luggage out of the trunk. She makes the quick walk around the corner to her building, the familiar sounds of the city replacing the sounds of the Cape. She pauses, looking up at the sign *Prince's Pastries and Catering*, before pushing open the front door.

Roseanne greets her with a warm hug. "Anthony left early. So, what is this idea of yours you have baking in your brain?"

"I'm home! Helloooo." She does a quick scan of the hallway as she drops her luggage then lets out a loud sigh.

Cody emerges from the kitchen, and instead of a warm hug or an "I missed you," he leans in to give her a quick peck on the cheek and steps back. "How was the drive?"

"Oh, it was uneventful. So, what's been going on?" she

asks as she walks toward the kitchen. She senses something, but she's not sure what.

"Nothing, absolutely nothing. I've been working on a new campaign logo, but there's nothing very exciting to update you on. I was just about to go to the gym, but I can skip it if you want to do something." Cody gives the impression he's guilty of something—hands in his pockets, no eye contact.

"Oh, didn't you get my text about when I'd be home? But never mind—of course, go to the gym. I've got a lot to catch up on."

Esme sits alone at her dining room table. A table they never use. *I wonder why we never eat here. Maybe we should start—eat dinner like normal people.* An oppressive silence hangs in the air. *I thought I'd feel great about being home and being with Cody. Everything I said about him, how I loved him, and our life together. I'm beginning to think that was just wishful thinking.* Her eyes dart around the room as if looking for anything that will bring her... whatever it is she's looking for. She stops, taking a moment to look out the large bay window. The view is classic Beacon Hill—brick sidewalks and federal-style architecture. Esme wants a different view. Esme wants a different life. She gets up slowly then brings her luggage to the bedroom to unpack.

"So, I haven't heard from CJ, have you?" she asks later, swirling her 2022 Chalk Hill Chardonnay and tapping her bare foot beneath the kitchen island.

"Nope. I guess, I hope, in this case silence is golden." Cody looks casually handsome, his wavy hair still wet from his shower.

"I've been thinking it might be cool for us to drive up the coast of Maine. You know, it might be fun to dip our toes somewhere other than the Atlantic Ocean. Spend an overnight to see CJ." She hates how her voice sounds needy —desperate—in her attempt to act normally.

"You do know that the coast of Maine is part of the Atlantic Ocean, right?"

Esme stares at Cody. *What the hell is wrong with you? Don't you see that our marriage is on very thin ice? Fucking-Atlantic-Ocean thin ice.* She gets up to pour herself more wine. *I guess I drank that fast.* She gestures to Cody, but he puts his hand up and shakes his head no.

"I'm still enjoying my first glass." He rolls his eyes and gives her a mocking look.

Esme is completely baffled by his attitude—she's usually the one being difficult.

"Is something wrong? You seem annoyed." She tilts her head to the left. "Have I done something to upset you? I'm confused because I don't see how that's possible. You went to the gym as soon as I got home. If anyone should be irked, I think it should be me."

"How about we start over from when you walked through the door after five days of no contact? Should we start there?" His words sound flat to her. His face is expressionless.

Esme twists a curl into a knot, looking at Cody as if she's seeing him for the first time.

"I don't understand what's happening right now. I'm lost. I cut my trip short to come home. I could have stayed longer," she lies. "I wasn't in touch because I was busy getting ready for the CBI wedding and then managing it on Saturday, and it went into the night."

Cody stands up, walks over to the bottle, and pours himself a refill, not bothering to ask Esme if she wants more.

"That's funny, about the wedding, because I asked Roseanne how it went, and she said it went smoothly—so smooth you could leave before it ended. She was genuinely happy that you could sneak out early to be with your friends." He leans against the counter and looks upward, shaking his head.

I will kill you, Roseanne. "It did go smoothly, just as it should. I said it went into the night, I didn't say I worked into the night. What the hell is going on, Cody?"

He raises both his hands. "I surrender, Esme. I'm done."

"You're done? Done with what?" she asks hesitantly, rubbing the back of her neck.

"I'm done with this charade of a marriage. I haven't felt like I'm part of a couple for..." He gives a long, low sigh, and his voice thickens. "Well, I don't know for how long. If I can't tell you that, then understand, I haven't felt much of anything for a very long time."

Esme is dumbstruck. She doesn't know what to say or to do. This time yesterday, she was on top of the world, the powerful rush of the waves roaring beneath her, feeling the exhilarating mix of freedom, fear, and simple, outright reckless fun. This time yesterday, Esme got her power back. Yet here she is, twenty-four hours later, listening to her husband tell her he is done, and she can feel her power slowly slipping away. *Say something. Say something!*

She's surprised by how her words sound in her shaky voice. "I-I-I don't have words. I don't know what to say. I'm completely and utterly baffled. What happened while I was gone to make you feel so, so—I don't know. I don't know what you're feeling, other than you say you're done. I need more to go on to figure this out. I can't go forward with those two words—you're done."

Cody runs his hand through his messy, damp hair, sending a brief twinge through Esme. He doesn't look at her. Instead, he turns his back to her and looks out the kitchen window.

"I noticed, when you were gone, that things weren't all that different. The only time it changed was when you would usually come home from the bakery. I spent that time doing what I wanted to do, not what you wanted to do."

He turned and put his hand up before she could barge in with a response. "I get it, you leave the house to go to work, and I don't. That's not my point." Again, his hand is up to stop Esme from interrupting. "Please let me talk. I might not have the strength to repeat myself."

Esme nods, reaching for her glass of wine, which, thankfully, isn't empty.

"My point is, I didn't miss you. I was surprised when I realized that—I don't miss Esme."

Those words sting, but she remains silent. She has both elbows on the marble island, her chin resting on her clasped hands. Esme avoids looking into his eyes, as if a simple glance from him will unleash the torrent of tears she's fighting to hold back.

But Cody isn't done. Esme's simple question—"What happened when I was gone?"—cracks open a vault of unspoken words and pent-up feelings, and a stream of emotions from the past nineteen years pours out of his mouth.

"I talked to Ethan the other day. He told me you were all there at the Pequod, just like old times. Everyone was there, even Delle." He seems to spit out Delle's name. "How do you think that made me feel? Everyone was there but me. You didn't tell me you'd be seeing Delle, or Ethan, for that matter. You told me it was a reunion of the E's." Cody's words are razor sharp, he's clearly agitated, and spittle is forming in the corners of his mouth. "You lied so I wouldn't come along and ruin your reunion with Delle."

Esme's earlier confusion is now teetering on contempt. She looks down and squeezes her eyes shut, taking a minute before speaking.

"Since when did you and Ethan start talking again? Ethan is a lying, cheating dirtbag. But if you want to rekindle your friendship with someone like that, don't let me stand in your way. And when did you become a conspiracy theorist? There was no conspiracy to keep you away from anything. I was there to spend time with Ellenor and Emma, my best friends, who I haven't seen in five years. Why on earth would you want to be a part of that? Not that I need to defend myself to you or anyone, but I say BS to your conspiracy theory. I did not know Ethan was on the Cape. It was our bad luck to run into him." She doesn't know what to do with her anger. Cody is on the other side of the island, leaving her stuck on the bar chair, feeling trapped.

"You said you were going to check on your mother's house. Did you even do that, or were you too busy hanging out with Delle?"

"Cody, you said you are done. Well, so am I, at least for right now." She wipes her nose with the back of her hand, still holding back tears, and gets up to move past Cody. She picks up her glass of wine and, as she is about to leave the room, Esme turns and looks at him, her eyes brimming with tears. "Life is funny, you know. This time yesterday, I was on top of the world, riding waves. Fast-forward twenty-four hours, and my husband is 'done with me.'"

As she walks down the hall, she hears, "You surfed?"

Safe in the sanctuary of her bathroom, Esme fills her tub, sobbing uncontrollably. She ties her hair up in a scrunchie and sinks into the hot water, hoping to scald the reality of what she has come home to out of her life.

The water has now gone cold, her tears have dried up, and she's out of wine. But in the time between scalding and cold, Esme has formulated a plan. Whether it works is yet to be seen.

"Good morning, Anthony."

"Well, it is a good morning, now that you're back." The heat of the ovens and Anthony's cheerful good morning has Esme smiling, and she feels a comforting warmth from head to toe.

Esme settles in with a cup of coffee and goes over the list for the day's orders. She leaves a message with her accountant to get in touch with her as soon as possible. The next call is to her attorney.

At seven, like clockwork, Roseanne pokes her head in the office door and says softly, "It's nice to have you back, boss."

Esme looks up. "Not sure how long you'll be calling me that, but thanks. It is nice to be back. Did you talk to your husband about my proposal?"

"I did. Tom and I talked a lot last night. I'll fill you in after the morning rush." She senses Esme's next question. "No need to pitch in, Abbey should be here any minute."

Later, Esme lets Roseanne and Anthony close up; she has better things to do. She walks up the stairs to her apartment—to her and Cody's apartment—as she has done more times than she cares to think about. Cody doesn't meet her at the door, which is unsettling. She doesn't want him to be there. *But why isn't he home?*

Chapter Twenty-Nine

"Love generally is a scary thing."
— Oksana Zabuzhko

Ellenor

"Good morning, and welcome to United Flight 791. We should be arriving in San Francisco right on schedule. The weather is a delightful seventy-one degrees with no rain in sight. Please sit back and enjoy the flight."

Ellenor looks out the window as the plane taxis down the runway. Once in the air, she orders a hot black coffee and pulls her journal out of her carry-on bag.

June somethingish. I have no clue what day this is. Holy crap, I survived another summer solstice with my tribe. We are small, but we are mighty. Man, we still love each other fiercely and fight as if our lives depend on being right. But that's allowed. Don't anyone dare try to mess with one of us—you will have the other two to deal with. Ethan messed with Emma. I wanted to rip his perfect head off of his perfect shoulders and dunk it in a vat of smelly fish heads, forever ruining his perfect hair. Delle seems to mess with everyone—I can't figure it out. I actually asked Esme if Delle was CJ's father. Holy shit, she came at me like nothing I've seen in years. Talk about pissed off, indignant, and maybe a bit... guilty? I don't know. Will I ever know? I get the impression that my brother has been having a great time amusing himself with my friends for years. I don't think it had occurred to me before this trip, but as tight as the three of us are, we keep secrets from each other. Esme spilled her guts about her marriage, and Emma was more subdued than usual. And I think Delle has something to do with that. But that's none of my business. None of this is my business, but it might be an interesting twist for another book. It was wonderful to be with Emma and Esme again. I don't know why we let so much time pass between visits. I drank too much and ate too much, but hey, I was on vacation. I'm proud of myself for standing up to Dad and the boys— that took balls, and I grew some that day. The first thing on the agenda when I'm home is to start work on buying the land from Dad. Well, not the first thing. Figuring out Maggie is the first thing. I'm so conflicted, and yes, I admit in this private journal that a lesbian relationship might be more than I can handle. I care deeply for Maggie. I might even love her. But how does that work in the real world? San Francisco isn't a problem. I don't think it would be a problem in most places. But I can't imagine bringing her to the Cape and introducing her to my family as my partner.

Imagine telling Dad she's my lover. Nope, not gonna happen, ever. And what if she comes on my next tour and we don't try to hide our relationship? Would that hurt, help, or have no impact on my readership? I wish I could be stronger and not care what people think. But I've seen how hurtful people can be. High school was brutal, and no adult stepped in to stop the bullying. Then again, I didn't tell any adult, not even my brothers. But I am talking about adults here. Those brothers of mine and the term 'adult' should be in the dictionary as the meaning of oxymoron. LOL. In fairness to friendship and secrets, I didn't tell Emma and Esme about Maggie right away. But in fairness to me, my feelings for her weren't apparent until Nantucket, so I didn't have a chance to tell them before that. I feel like I'm standing at a crossroads, torn between resistance and hope.

Ellenor puts down the pen and stares out the window. The sky is a vast blanket of varying shades of gray, with hints of sunlight and blue poking through. *It's beyond the scope of my imagination to grasp the vastness of the sky. Where do the shades of gray merge into blue? Reminds me of the ocean. Do the colors end on the horizon, or do they go on for infinity?*

She's woken up with "Welcome to San Francisco. It's a balmy seventy-eight degrees, with no precipitation in sight. Enjoy your visit to the City by the Bay. If you are passing through, please check for your next flight information as you disembark from the plane. It will be to your right."

Ellenor moves along, following the throngs of people

heading to baggage claim. She feels the calm she experienced on the plane slowly evaporate, irritation pushing in to take over. While waiting for her luggage, she checks her emails and texts. Most are spam, except one—one from Jill.

> I'm outside in lot C. Text me when you
> get to the sidewalk.

Ellenor smiles. *Good old Jill. Good old, dependable Jill. I wonder what her story is. I don't know anything about her.*

Ellenor feels a wave of nausea wash over her, her heart begins pounding in her chest, and she realizes she's perspiring as she reaches for one of her bags on the turnstile. She pulls the bag off and drags it off to the side, away from the crowd of travelers. *Holy crap, am I having a heart attack?* She hopes not to attract any attention. She finds a seat and places her oversized suitcase in front of her to rest her head on. Ellenor fumbles for a tissue to wipe the sweat off her forehead and focuses on taking deep breaths—in for four seconds, hold for seven seconds, exhale for eight seconds. *How the hell do I know how to do that?* In minutes, her heartbeat returns to a normal pace, and the nausea is gone. Ellenor takes one more deep breath, composing herself before gathering her remaining luggage and maneuvering the bags out to the busy sidewalk.

Once outside, she texts Jill a simple "I'm here." With her eyes closed, she tilts her head up, enjoying the sun's warmth on her face while blocking out the sounds of airport traffic. *So different from the Cape.*

"Ellenor! Over here. Hurry—I'm illegally double

parked." Jill runs to the back of her car to open the trunk. "Welcome back."

"Oh, thanks. It's good to be back, I think." She fastens her seatbelt, acutely aware that what happened to her in the airport isn't normal.

"How did you know when to pick me up?"

"Maggie told me. She asked that I pick you up. Ubers can knock out the Zen from a vacation faster than a speeding ticket."

Ellenor laughs. "I never heard that one before. I'll be sure to thank Maggie." Glancing over at Jill, it hits her. *Does Jill know? And if so, what does she know? Would she care if Maggie and I were a couple? Would that ruin everything? I can't do this. I can't.* The wave of nausea returns, along with her racing heart.

"Are you okay?" Jill asks, her eyes quickly darting from the road, a worried frown furrowing her brow.

Ellenor is ashen white, even with her tan, and her breathing is ragged. She raises her hand as if to dismiss what is obviously happening. "Yeah, yeah, I'm fine. Just feeling a little off. Probably something I ate on the plane."

In for four seconds, hold for seven seconds, exhale for eight seconds. During the hold for seven seconds, she texts her doorman.

> Arriving soon—would like help with my luggage.

Once inside her condo, Ellenor slides her back down the door and sits still, trying to grasp what happened and why it happened. She stays like this, silent, eyes closed, until her breath returns to normal.

Her cell dings. She doesn't know where it is, and she doesn't care. After what seems like an eternity, Ellenor gets up off the floor and focuses on her surroundings. *I'm home. I'm home.* She steps around the pile of luggage, pours herself a large glass of water, then sinks onto the couch.

What am I going to do? It doesn't take a trained therapist to tell me I had an all-out, full-blown panic attack at the airport. But why? Sipping her water, she retraces what was happening before she panicked. *I was waiting for the rest of my luggage. Nobody was bugging me. I got the text from Jill— bingo. I freaked out thinking about what would happen if Jill found out about me and Maggie.* She gets up and begins walking around the living room, tapping her temple with her index and middle fingers. *This can't be good. If I have this kind of reaction simply thinking about someone, especially someone as familiar as Jill, knowing Maggie and I are only considering a relationship, how can I face the rest of the world?*

She continues to pace and tap her temple. *Think, think. Okay, Esme and Emma. I told them, and I didn't panic. So maybe it's ok to be upfront with the world. But shit, the world is full of cruel people.* Her stomach turns, causing her to sit and close her eyes. *Breathe, just breathe. I've gotten this far in life, and I've done plenty of gossip-worthy stuff. What's one more scandal on my resume? But nothing I've done has brought on a panic attack. I can't do this if this is the reaction my body has. How do I get a grip? Or maybe I don't get a grip and give up on the idea that I might be in love with Maggie.*

Ellenor's cell dings again, pulling her out of her slide

down the what-if rabbit hole. She takes a big sip of water and follows the sound of her phone, which she finds in that silly purse Maggie insisted she get. The text is from Joseph, the doorman. Does she need anything? She smiles. Joseph is a big teddy bear of a man who could easily kick someone to the curb while personally delivering a bag of cold remedies from the pharmacy. Ellenor texts him a happy face emoji.

> Thanks, but I am all set. 😊

She then sees the text she missed earlier, the one that she heard while she was sitting on the floor, trying to figure out how to get up and function.

> Welcome home! Jill let me know she got you there in one piece. She mentioned you looked a little pale, maybe coming down with something. I hope it's only a touch of jet lag. Let me know if you need anything. I will drop everything and come right over. Or merely let me know if you're ok. Talk soon, M.

Ellenor takes a few minutes, trying to figure out how to respond. She feels the weight of the day's events pressing down on her, leaving her utterly exhausted. Her day began as the sun was rising, a sharp contrast to her typical wake-up time, but Callahan Cottage is a good two hours from Logan Airport. She had to return her rental car and catch a flight from the Cape to Logan in the hopes of beating the clock and making her connecting flight home. All of this before ten in the morning. *These are legit reasons why I don't want to see Maggie—I'm exhausted. Or is that the root of why my emotions are on overdrive? Maybe I don't want to see her.*

> Hi—thanks for sending in the cavalry to save me from an Uber. I'm exhausted. Long day. Let's catch up tomorrow.

Send.

Ellenor closes every blind and shade in her condo and carefully places Avril Lavigne's *Let Go* album on her ancient turntable. She pours another large glass of water and walks into her bathroom. Once the tub is full, she undresses and steps in, slowly sinking into the hot water. Ellenor stretches out in the large free-standing tub, closes her eyes, stops her mind from spinning, and quietly sings along with the haunting melody of "I'm With You."

Chapter Thirty

Female friendship was one-tenth prevention
and nine-tenths cleanup."
— Maggie Shipstead

Winter Solstice

Ellenor glances at her watch and smiles. "I need to answer this. You keep reading—I'll catch up. Anyway, I know how it ends."

Maggie removes her oversized red-rimmed reading glasses and smiles at Ellenor. "It might be a different ending by the time you get back."

Ellenor pours herself a glass of champagne and walks toward the bedroom, but on second thought, she brings the bottle of Moët in with her. She snuggles up in her king-size bed, leaning against the navy blue upholstered headboard, and takes a sip before logging on to the video call. The champagne rests on the back of her throat as she says, "We did it. Another solstice, another year."

"Happy Winter Solstice! Does everyone have a glass of champagne?"

"Of course we do, Esme," the other two answer.

"Okay, who goes first this year?" Emma asks.

"I think it's my turn to go first this year." Esme has also taken her bottle of Dom Pérignon into her bedroom and is settled on the upholstered window seat overlooking Beacon Hill and the Boston Common.

"You say that every year, Esme. And we always give in. Well, not this year, my dear." Emma is sitting on her sofa under a cashmere throw, champagne at the ready, as she watches the first snowflakes of the season begin to fall outside her window.

Ignoring Emma, Esme says, "I don't think I'll ever tire of how tranquil Boston is during the holidays. It helps me to stop hating most people and work toward goodwill to all men, or something like that."

Across the country, Ellenor laughs. "San Francisco isn't looking too festive today—it's cold and rainy, but we've got it going on inside here."

Emma smiles, sipping her champagne. "Okay, looks like Ellenor has the talking stick. What's got it going on inside?"

"Maggie is what's going on. It's miserable outside, but the house is cozy, the fire is lit, and we're both reading what I hope is the last draft of my new book."

"Shut up!" screams Esme.

"Spill!" yells Emma.

"What do you want first? Book? Or Maggie?"

"We want everything," Esme says.

Ellenor takes a sip and cautiously begins to fill Esme and Emma in on what has been going on in her world.

"I don't want to jinx anything, but I think I can safely

say that everything seems to be falling into place. Maggie and I are at a good point in our relationship. We're still learning our way around each other, but it's really nice to have a genuine connection with someone. I love the feeling of belonging, which is something I've only felt with you two. And speaking of feelings, I have a good one about this book, number freaking eleven. Do you believe that? I have been binge-writing this story. I don't think I've ever been as focused on any writing as I have been with this one. Usually, I'm a sloppy mess when I'm about to publish something, but this time, I'm confident. This is the best writing I've ever done, and I'm damn proud of it."

"I've never doubted your talent. You keep getting stronger and more creative with each book. I can't wait to read this one. What's the title? But first fill us in on Maggie. Tell us everything. Are you guys exclusive? Are you living together? Either way, I'm all Team Maggie."

"Thank you for the Maggie endorsement, Emma. I'm all Team Maggie too. We are exclusive, as you put it, but we're not living together. It's too soon. We both love our places and our privacy, and I can't function without my quiet time. It's working for now, and I'm not rocking this boat. Oh, and the title is *When We Were Mermaids*. I can't wait for you both to read it. Okay, who's next?"

"Me, I'm next. Sorry, Esme. So, what's been going on in my life since we talked? You both know about the end of E&G.

Yesterday was the last photo shoot of the year. I am done, baby."

"And now what? Maybe travel the world?"

"World travel isn't in the cards at this moment, Ellenor. Unless some famously rich dog lovers fly me to Italy to photograph their dogs." Emma's enthusiasm is bubbling over through the video call, east to west.

"That sounds fantastic—but dogs? How did this come about?" Esme asks, even though she's undoubtedly chomping on the bit to share her news.

"It hit me when we were at the cottage in June. I had a complete meltdown after that fabulous lunch with Ben."

"Who?" Ellenor asks, pouring more Moët into her flute.

"Ben Maloney. Remember that handsome running guy on the beach?" Emma's tone has a hint of annoyance.

"Okay, I remember, don't get your panties in a bunch. Unless, of course, someone has been doing that for you."

"I hate you, Ellenor," Emma says with a laugh. "After I rudely left him, I found myself parked on the side of the road by the cove, bawling my eyes out. I saw a woman with her dogs on the beach—nobody else, just them. It was sheer magic watching those dogs running on the sand, charging into the water, not a care in the world other than the tennis ball. Long story short, I stopped crying and asked her if I could snap a few pictures. I ran alongside Johnny and June, chasing them into the water and having more fun than I'd had in years."

"Who are Johnny and June? Sounds like Johnny Cash and June Carter. Did you freaking meet Johnny Cash on the beach and not tell us?" Now it's Esme's energy coming through the screen, all fired up, demanding more.

Emma throws her head back in laughter. *God, I love these two crazy women.* "No, of course not. Johnny and June are Cape Cod black dogs. Those two silly dogs taught me something my soul grabbed onto, as tight as June with her stick. They taught me to remember who I am and to be my authentic self. I left that beach with a newfound sense of confidence. Some people say things like 'they found themselves.' Maybe they did. But for me, I didn't find myself—I unquestionably found another version of myself. This is a version of Emma Callahan who's not beholden to anyone. I've unearthed a zest for life that I haven't felt in years. And ladies, it feels fantastic!"

"It's about time," Ellenor says, raising her glass. "Toast to Emma and to next year—the year of the dog." Ellenor laughs a genuine laugh, clearly thrilled for Emma and her next chapter.

"Year of the dog—that's a good one. Toast to Emma." Esme raises her glass as well, feeling a warm comfort wash over her. *I am eternally grateful to have these people in my life.*

"You're up, Esme. We want every juicy detail of what's been going on in your life. Where's Cody, how's CJ handling the separation, how are *you* handling the separation?"

"How much time have you got?" Esme asks. She takes a minute to think before jumping in.

"Okay, yeah, there are a lot of moving parts right now. You both already know how crushed I was after my marriage spiraled down the toilet. When I left the Cape after the solstice, I had convinced myself that I was in love with Cody. But I wasn't. And he wasn't in love with me. It's funny—we do love each other, but we aren't in love. There's a big difference between the two.

"I think it was one of the hardest things I've ever done —call it quits, even though I was unhappy being married. I took a leap of faith and rented a cottage in Wells, Maine. I needed to be alone and wrap my head around what was happening. I picked Wells since it has good waves and great beaches, but it would also give me a chance to figure out why my kid loved spending the summer on the coast of Maine. My little cottage on the beach was a perfect retreat for me. I surfed a lot, thought a lot, and took the time to get to know myself. I hadn't been alone, really alone, in twenty years. And before anyone asks, Cody is doing good. I think he's also getting to know himself. He's in therapy, and I know he will end up where he's supposed to be. I know we both will.

"The sale of the bakery went smoothly, although it took longer than I wanted. But it's done. I'm confident Roseanne and Anthony will be successful as the new owners. They both have such passion and drive, and I'm rooting for them. I'm going to do contract work with them, but only when I want to. As Emma said, I'm not beholden to anyone. The money from the sale paid off the mortgage on this place, so I'm keeping the apartment. The bakery will pay rent, which will help with Cody and me living separately. His apartment is stupidly expensive, but that's typical in Boston. CJ is spending his winter break here with us, and I'm loving every minute."

Ellenor interrupts. "You and Cody are separated, so what do you mean when you say CJ's spending his winter break with both of you?"

"Just that. CJ is our kid, and we both want to be with him. Cody and I are still working hard on ourselves—separately, of course, but when it comes to supporting CJ, we come together as a team. It's rather refreshing, considering the alternative. Both of us recognize we sucked at being husband and wife, but we rock at being mom and dad. So that's where I am right now. I feel good about the future, especially since I'm heading to Maui on the twenty-sixth. CJ is coming a week later, and we are going to spend as much time surfing as possible. That's it for me. What are your guys doing for Christmas?"

"I'm planning a low-key nothing day. Probably no different from any other day." Ellenor says flatly.

Esme chooses her words carefully, a technique she is working on with her therapist. "That sounds like it might be a refreshing change from the stress holidays can bring on."

"What about Maggie?" Emma blurts out.

Ellenor squirms on her bed, trying to not spill her champagne. In a lower voice, she says, "Maggie is going home for Christmas. Obviously, I'm not going back home. It's fine, you guys. It's only a day. Not a big deal. Seriously."

Emma and Esme don't react immediately.

Why isn't she going with Maggie? "I have an idea. Why

don't you join me in Maui? I rented a three-bedroom bungalow right on the beach, and I'm alone for the first week. But you can stay as long as you want. I'm there for the month of January. Come on, it will be fun. CJ would love to spend some time with you."

A brief spark runs across Ellenor's face. "Why not? I might take you up on that, Esme. I'm sure there are direct flights out of SFO. Let me look into it."

"What about you, Emma? What are your plans?"

"I'm pretending tomorrow is Christmas Day in New York. Ben's coming into the city. We are going to do it all in one day—skate at Rockefeller Center and hit the Winter Village at Bryant Park. It is the best Christmas market. If you ever have a chance, check it out. We haven't figured out where to have lunch, but probably someplace around Bryant Park. Then we have tickets to see the Rockettes in the afternoon. We'll have some time to kill before we grab a cab over to Pier 62 for the Manhattan holiday yacht cruise. I'm looking forward to that. It's a holiday light cruise that sails through New York Harbor on a 1920s-style yacht. I'm exhausted just talking about it." Emma's enthusiasm is contagious.

Esme asks, "Are you seeing Ben?"

"We are seeing each other, not a lot, but yes, we are."

Emma's coy response causes Esme to sit up at attention. "Really? When did this start up? Like you said, the last time you saw him, you were horribly rude. What about the red flags?"

"Don't remind me. I called him a few days after I got home from the Cape. I swallowed my pride, begged forgiveness, and asked what I could do to make it up to him. Within reason, of course. He said the only way he could look beyond what I did was if I would go to a Yankees-Sox game and openly support the Yankees."

"Ugh" is the response from both Ellenor and Esme.

"I said okay. No matter how much it hurt, I would do it." She laughs. "It was so much fun and also humiliating. He made me buy a Yankees baseball cap and wear that and an old New York Yankees shirt of his for the entire day. Ben even booked us a group tour of Yankee Stadium and let everyone know I was a rabid Red Sox fan. But I did it all with grace and dignity, and we've been casually seeing each other since. But my red flag radar is on high alert when I'm with him. I've got this under control." She empties her glass and reaches for more champagne. "As for Christmas, I fly to London on the twenty-third to spend Christmas with Grace and Dave. I'm looking forward to seeing them. I miss Grace. But I also want to experience a traditional English Christmas, whatever that is. It should be a 'jolly good time,'" Emma says, attempting a British accent.

"My bottle has run dry, so perhaps it's time to say good-bye." Esme hiccups, pleased with her spur-of-the-moment rhyme.

"Same here, almost gone. But before I leave, let's remember what the winter solstice is about. It's the longest night of the year, a reminder of how darkness must exist before dawn can break through, bringing in light, leaving our issues and baggage behind. We have each had one hell of a year, good and bad. Let's keep on moving toward the good."

"Well said, Ellenor. I wish for joy, love, and peace, not only for us and our loved ones, but for the world," Emma says reflectively.

"Love you all. Happy solstice, happy Christmas, and wishing us the best new year. Bye." Esme smiles as she ends the call. *See you soon, mermaids.*

The End

About the Author

Judy Lannon's award-winning contemporary women's fiction resonates with readers through its honest and relatable depiction of women and their life experiences.

A conversation with a friend inspired Judy to write her debut novel, *Nine Days*, which won multiple awards soon after publication, launching her writing career.

Her books have been recognized by the American Writers Association for Best New Debut Fiction and Best Women's Fiction, the Firebird Book Awards, and the New York City Big Book Award.

Judy lives and writes at her home on Cape Cod, Massachusetts, close to the Atlantic Ocean. Though she thinks it's a cliché to say the ocean inspires her, she happily accepts that label since it's a constant presence in her writing and her life.

If you would like to know more about Judy, her books, and book club events, please visit her website, www.AuthorJudyLannon.com

Please follow her on social media:
Facebook: tinyurl.com/ybuptb34
Instagram: @judylannonofficial
Amazon: tinyurl.com/4359ys8r

Quotes and Notes

I enjoy adding quotes to the start of each chapter. I feel it gives a subtle hint of what is coming. With *Callahan's Cottage*, I'd like to share some background on the famous people who spoke these words, including a peek at some captivating stories and their impact on history. As I dug into their backgrounds, I became fascinated by their unique personalities, pasts, and present lives.

These quotes, from Winne-the-Pooh's gentle wisdom to the profound depth of James Baldwin, represent a treasure trove of lives lived beyond what many of us can imagine.

Who knew that in 1927, Dorothy Parker was fined $5 for "sauntering" in a Boston demonstration or that, in her will, she left the bulk of her estate to Reverend Dr. Martin Luther King Jr.? I had never heard of Goethe before I came across his quote. After doing some research on him, I need to know more about this man.

I went deep down a rabbit hole on some of these

quotes. For example, in *The Lion King*, Rafiki is considered a source of profound wisdom and inspiration. Through his sage advice and memorable quotes, Rafiki teaches valuable lessons about life, love, and the importance of embracing our true selves.

Ellenor Roosevelt was, in her time, one of the world's most widely admired and powerful women.

Elbert Hubbard was convicted on one count of circulating "objectionable" matter in violation of the postal law, received a presidential pardon, and died with the sinking of the *Lusitania* in 1915.

Chapter One

"I hate writing, I love having written." Dorothy Parker was an American poet and writer of fiction, plays, and screenplays based in New York. She was known for her caustic wisecracks and eye for 20th-century urban foibles.

Chapter Two

"Everything is hard before it is easy." Johann Wolfgang von Goethe was a German polymath who is widely regarded as the greatest and most influential writer in the German language.

Chapter Three

"This isn't working out the way I was hoping!" Tigger is a

fictional character in A.A. Milne's *Winnie-the-Pooh* books and their adaptations.

Chapter Four

"Time doesn't take away from friendship, nor does separation." Tennessee Williams was an American playwright and screenwriter. He is considered among the three foremost playwrights of 20th-century American drama.

Chapter Five

"Embrace uncertainty. Some of the most beautiful chapters in our lives won't have a title until much later." Bob Goff is an American lawyer, speaker, and author of *The New York Times* best-selling books *Love Does* and *Everybody, Always*.

Chapter Six

"Not everything that is faced can be changed, but nothing can be changed until it is faced." James Baldwin was a gay Black man in America and the grandson of a slave. He used his upbringing to inspire individuals through his words in novels, essays, and plays.

Chapter Seven

"There is nothing to writing. All you do is sit down at a typewriter and bleed." Ernest Hemingway was an American novelist, short-story writer, and journalist who has been romanticized for his adventurous lifestyle and outspoken, blunt public image.

Chapter Eight

"We all have big changes in our lives that are more or less a second chance." Harrison Ford is an American actor and is regarded as a cinematic cultural icon.

Chapter Nine

"But when alcohol comes in, start running. Because there's a demon there, and it goes back to her childhood." David Gest was an American producer and television personality who founded the American Cinema Awards Foundation in 1983.

Chapter Ten

"The past can hurt, but the way I see it you can either run from it or learn from it." Rafiki is the wise sage and shaman who guides Mufasa, Simba, and more through their experiences and struggles in *The Lion King*.

Chapter Eleven

"Stop worrying about missed opportunities and start looking for new ones." Im Chang-kyun, known by the stage name I.M, is a South Korean rapper, singer, songwriter, and producer.

Chapter Twelve

"The most beautiful discovery true friends make is that they can grow separately without growing apart." Elisabeth Grace Foley is the author of numerous works of historical fiction and historical mystery set mostly in the American West.

Chapter Thirteen

"We didn't even realize we were making memories; we just knew we were having fun." Winnie-the-Pooh was named after a teddy bear owned by A.A. Milne's son, Christopher Robin Milne, on whom the character Christopher Robin was based.

Chapter Fourteen

"Summer is always the best of what might be." Charles Bowden was an author and journalist acclaimed for his vivid, unsparing, and often lyrical portrayals of life in the Southwest.

Chapter Fifteen

"There's nothing more beautiful than the way the ocean refuses to stop kissing the shoreline, no matter how many times it's sent away." Sarah Kay is an American poet known for her spoken word poetry and is the founder of Project VOICE, a group dedicated to using spoken word as an educational and inspirational tool.

Chapter Sixteen

"I had a very dysfunctional family, and a very hard childhood. So I made a world out of words. And it was my salvation." Mary Oliver was an American poet who won the National Book Award and the Pulitzer Prize. She found inspiration for her work in nature and had a lifelong habit of solitary walks in the wild.

Chapter Seventeen

"Planning is the art of pretending you have control over the universe." Alan W. Watts was a British and American writer, speaker, and self-styled "philosophical entertainer" known for interpreting and popularizing Buddhist, Taoist, and Hindu philosophy for a Western audience.

Chapter Eighteen

"Some things are so unexpected that no one is prepared for them." Leo Rosten was an American writer and humorist in the fields of scriptwriting, story-writing, journalism, and Yiddish lexicography.

Chapter Nineteen

"Friends give you a shoulder to cry on. But best friends are ready with a shovel to hurt the person that made you cry." Unknown is unknown, but I would like to meet them!

Chapter Twenty

"I am who I am today because of the choices I made yesterday." Eleanor Roosevelt was an American political figure, diplomat, and activist. She was the longest serving first lady of the United States.

Chapter Twenty-One

"It's possible to go on, no matter how impossible it seems." Nicholas Sparks is an American novelist, screenwriter, and film producer.

Chapter Twenty-Two

"Life moves on and so should we." Spencer Johnson is one of the world's most influential thinkers and beloved authors.

Chapter Twenty-Three

"You are one decision away from a completely different life." Mel Robbins is an American author, motivational speaker, and podcast host.

Chapter Twenty-Four

"To move forward, you have to leave the past behind." Susannah Cahalan is an American writer and author known for writing the memoir *Brain on Fire: My Month of Madness*.

Chapter Twenty-Five

"Nothing soothes the soul like a walk on a Cape Cod beach." Unknown must love the Cape beaches as much as I do.

Chapter Twenty-Six

"A friend is someone who knows all about you and loves you just the same." Elbert Hubbard was an American writer, publisher, artist, and philosopher.

Chapter Twenty-Seven

"A friend is someone who gives you total freedom to be yourself." Jim Morrison was the lead vocalist for The Doors.

Chapter Twenty-Eight

"Friendship has splendors that love knows not." Mariama Bâ was a Senegalese author and feminist whose two French-language novels were translated into more than a dozen languages.

Chapter Twenty-Nine

"Love generally is a scary thing." Oksana Zabuzhko is a contemporary Ukrainian writer, poet, and essayist.

Chapter Thirty

"Female friendship was one-tenth prevention and nine-tenths cleanup." Maggie Shipstead is *The New York Times* bestselling author of three novels and a short story collection.

www.ingramcontent.com/pod-product-compliance
Lightning Source LLC
Chambersburg PA
CBHW021418110726
47901CB00008B/2203